THE HARDY BOYS

UNDERCOVER BROTHERS

#6 **Burned**

FRANKLIN W. DIXON

Aladdin Paperbacks
New York   London   Toronto   Sydney

THE HARDY BOYS
UNDERCOVER BROTHERS™

#1 *Extreme Danger* #4 *Thrill Ride*

#2 *Running on Fumes* #5 *Rocky Road*

#3 *Boardwalk Bust* #6 *Burned*

Available from Simon & Schuster

This book is a work of fiction. Any references to historical events, real people, or real locales are used fictitiously. Other names, characters, places, and incidents are the product of the author's imagination, and any resemblance to actual events or locales or persons, living or dead, is entirely coincidental.

☞ ALADDIN PAPERBACKS
An imprint of Simon & Schuster, Children's Publishing Division,
1230 Avenue of the Americas, New York, NY 10020

THE HARDY BOYS MYSTERY STORIES and HARDY BOYS UNDER-COVER BROTHERS are trademarks of Simon & Schuster, Inc.
ALADDIN PAPERBACKS and colophon are trademarks of Simon & Schuster, Inc.
Designed by Lisa Vega
The text of this book was set in Aldine 401BT.
Manufactured in the United States of America
First Aladdin Paperbacks edition October 2005
10 9 8 7 6 5 4

Library of Congress Control Number: 2005921360
ISBN-13: 978-1-4169-0008-5
ISBN-10: 1-4169-0008-X

TABLE OF CONTENTS

1. SSSSSSSSS! 1
2. *Jaws of Death* 11
3. *Surprise Packages* 19
4. *Top 40 Suspects* 30
5. *Dodging Questions* 40
6. *The Web of Crime* 50
7. *Money to Burn* 58
8. *Mega Madness* 68
9. *Shop Till You Drop (Dead)* 78
10. *The Mysterious Mr. Burns* 88
11. *Playing with Fire* 98
12. *Burned!* 109
13. *To the Bitter End* 116
14. *Band on the Run* 126
15. *Dead or Alive* 134
16. *Facing the Music* 144

1.

SSSSSSSSS!

I heard the hissing sound first.

Then I saw it slither out of its cage.

Easy, dude.

I stopped in my tracks and held my breath. The creature moved so fast I could only make out a blur of gray scales uncoiling at my feet. In two seconds flat, the reptile reared up in front of me—and locked eyes with mine.

Hello.

It was "The King." And I'm not talking about Elvis Presley.

This was a king cobra. Twelve feet of angry, hissing poison with beady yellow eyes, a big flaring hood, and a glistening pair of needle-sharp fangs.

I kid you not.

1

"Don't move, Joe."

My brother Frank lay on the floor in the corner, next to a smelly tank of baby turtles. I was glad to see that he was okay. Outback Mack had clobbered him pretty good with a twenty-pound bag of pet feed.

Yes, *the* Outback Mack.

You may have seen his hokey homemade commercials on late-night TV. "G'day, mates," he'd drawl in his exaggerated Australian accent. "I'm Outback Mack. And if you like rare and exotic animals as much as I do, you'll just love Outback Mack's Animal Shack. We've got snakes, turtles, iguanas, gators, you name it . . . all in one convenient location off Route 17." Then he'd cock his pith helmet, hold up a lizard, and wink. "You gotta love 'em."

What a creep.

If he loved rare and exotic animals so much, why would he ship them into the country illegally, packed into filthy crates as if they were office supplies?

Outback Mack was a criminal, no doubt about it.

Which is why Frank and I were assigned to this case.

Let me explain. My brother and I are undercover agents for ATAC—American Teens Against Crime—and we applied for after-school jobs at Outback Mack's so we could gather evidence of illegal wildlife trading. The United States has strict laws about importing and selling exotic animals, and Outback Mack was breaking every rule in the book. The fool even thought he could advertise his business on television without getting caught.

But Frank and I underestimated him.

Outback Mack had figured out who we were and what we were doing. He caught my brother going through his files—and that's when he clubbed him with a big bag of pet feed.

And—oh, yeah—that's when he unleashed the king cobra.

Nice guy.

I could hear Outback Mack's footsteps as he dashed down a corridor and out of the warehouse.

I could also hear the king cobra . . . hissing at me.

"Stay calm, Joe," Frank whispered.

Was he kidding? There I was, face-to-face with a giant killer reptile, and my oh-so-thoughtful brother wanted me to stay calm?

Yeah, right. No problem, bro.

The cobra flared its hood even wider.

"This is not cool, Frank," I managed to gasp. "He's getting ready to strike."

"Just relax. King cobras aren't usually aggressive. They tend to flee."

"Really? Tell *him* that."

"Don't make any sudden moves."

"I'm not planning to."

"Just hold still and I'll call for backup."

Frank slowly pulled his cell phone from his jacket pocket and speed-dialed the local police. I stood there like a statue, frozen by the cold stare of the king cobra.

If looks could kill . . .

Those eyes were the scariest things I'd ever seen—except maybe for those fangs.

What are you looking at, snake? Your next lunch?

A pink forked tongue darted in and out of the cobra's mouth. I couldn't help but wonder what I looked like through the eyes of a snake. A super-sized cheeseburger? An extra-tall order of fries?

"Help is on the way," said Frank, clicking off his phone.

"Great," I replied. "But what if Mr. Hissy here bites me before they arrive?"

Frank took a deep breath. "Actually, king cobras aren't as venomous as smaller cobras."

"So I wouldn't die?"

Frank hesitated. "Well, um, probably. One bite delivers enough venom to bring down an elephant . . . or twenty men."

"Thanks for the fun facts, Mr. Discovery Channel."

The snake hissed at the sound of my voice.

"Quiet, Joe," my brother whispered. "I have an idea."

"It better be a good one."

"It's the only one I got."

"That's good enough for me."

Frank rose slowly to his feet. "You have your CD player with you, right?"

"Sure," I answered. "It's in my back pocket. Why? Do you want to groove on some tunes while I die? Go ahead, check out the new Thrasher CD. That should drown out my screams."

"Maybe the music will distract the cobra," Frank explained. "It works for snake charmers."

"But dude," I protested, staring at the hooded reptile in front of me. "I don't see any ears on this guy."

"Believe it or not, snakes have a highly developed sense of hearing."

"Speak up, Frank. I don't think the killer snake heard you."

My brother ignored me. "Their ears are internal. They feel the sound vibrations in their jaws."

I stared at the cobra's powerful jaws and shuddered. "So where do we put the headphones? On his fangs?"

"I think he'll be able to hear it across the room."

5

"You *think*?"

"Just stand still, Joe. I'll creep up behind you and get the CD player. Then I'll try to lure the snake away with the music."

I sighed. "Try real hard."

"Don't worry, man. I got your back."

"Unfortunately, the snake's got my front."

"Shhhhh."

Out of the corner of my eye, I watched Frank sneak up behind me, moving so slowly and silently that the king cobra didn't seem to notice.

I'm the one that he wants.

The giant reptile moved its head closer to mine— less than two feet away—and hissed at me again.

Hey, buddy. Say it, don't spray it.

Then he fixed those cold, hungry eyes on me. My heart pounded so loudly in my chest, the snake probably heard it with those internal ears of his.

Maybe I'll die of a heart attack instead of a snake bite.

Something bumped me from behind.

It's got me!

But no. It was Frank, reaching into my back pocket and pulling out my CD player. I let out a little sigh of relief.

Then I remembered something. Something bad.

"Frank?"

"I'm right behind you, bro."

"The batteries are almost dead."

Frank didn't say anything. He simply stepped back and moved slowly to the corner of the room. Then he clicked a button on the CD player and waited.

Nothing. No music, just silence.

I'm snake food.

Frank turned the volume dial. I held my breath.

Come on, batteries.

A soft burst of heavy metal music erupted from the tiny earphones.

All right!

The cobra stopped hissing and turned its head toward the CD player. I grinned at Frank.

It's working, dude!

Slowly the giant snake swerved its entire body, inching its way closer to the sound.

"He hears it," said Frank. "And I think he likes it."

"I told you, this new CD totally rocks."

The snake slithered across the floor and reared up in front of my brother. Its hood flared open, its head swaying gently back and forth.

"Look at him," said Frank. "He's hypnotized by the music."

"Yeah," I agreed. "And he's got you trapped in a corner. Now what? Do you have a Plan B?"

Frank glanced over his shoulder toward the back wall of the warehouse. Then he turned around and gazed at the door leading out of the room.

"I have an idea," he said, slowly crouching down. "I'm going to slide the CD player across the floor toward the back wall. When the snake goes after it, we run for the door. You go first. I'll try to shut the door on my way out."

I frowned. "Sounds risky."

"Do you have a problem with that?"

"Are you kidding? Risky is my middle name."

"I thought it was Irving."

"Are we going to do this or not?"

Frank nodded grimly and squatted down, placing the CD player on the floor. The king cobra held its focus on the earphones. It angled its head downward, ready to strike at any second.

That's when the batteries died.

No!

The music stopped. And the snake hissed.

"Frank!" I shouted.

The cobra's head spun around. It glared at me with those angry yellow eyes.

Frank slammed the CD player against the floor. The sound of static crackled through the earphones.

Music! Yes!

A heavy metal guitar solo flowed from the small plastic player—and captured the attention of the snake. The cobra swung around and glared at Frank.

With a quick shove, Frank sent the CD player sliding to the back wall.

The king cobra sprang after it, jaws open, fangs glistening.

In a flash it shot past Frank's foot. And sank its teeth intol the CD player.

"Run!"

I bolted for the doorway. Frank was right behind me. Sliding into the hall, I turned to see Frank grabbing the doorknob.

The king cobra slithered after us. Fast.

Slam!

The door closed with a bang—followed by a loud thump.

"Ouch," I said. "It sounds like Mr. Snake bumped his head."

"I think he'll be okay. Now let's get out of here and see if we can find Outback Mack."

Frank and I turned to face a long hallway lined with animal cages of all shapes and sizes.

"Um, Frank," I said softly. "Do you see what I see?"

My brother looked and nodded.

Outback Mack must have opened all the cages on his way out of the building.

The entire hallway was crawling with animals.

Snakes, turtles, lizards, iguanas, alligators—if they

were slimy or slithering, they were there. Dozens and dozens of reptiles and amphibians from all over the world were crammed into one long narrow space—right between us and the exit door.

"How do we get out of this one, Frank?" I whispered.

My brother smiled. "Very carefully."

Without a trace of hesitation, he started walking down the hall, careful not to step on any of the creepy crawlers.

Is he crazy?

A red-and-black-striped snake hissed at me from the top of a cage. I sighed and followed in my brother's footsteps.

"Don't worry, Joe," he told me. "Most of these animals can't kill you."

"*Most* of them?" I asked. "What about the others?"

"If they bite you, you die."

"Thanks for clearing that up."

I watched Frank step over a four-foot-long alligator without batting an eye.

Well, if he can do it, I can do it.

Taking a deep breath, I marched ahead.

And got bit by a baby iguana.

2.

Jaws of Death

"Get it off of me! Get it off of me!"

Joe kept shouting and shaking his foot, but the little iguana just wouldn't let go of his pant leg.

I started laughing.

"It's not funny, Frank!"

"It sure *looks* funny, Joe."

Ignoring my comment, my brother pushed me out of the way and charged out of the warehouse, leaping over lizards and snakes like they were hurdles at a track meet.

I followed him outside.

"Let go! Let go of me!"

Joe hopped up and down in the parking lot, banging into a road sign for Outback Mack's Animal

Shack. The iguana dangled from his thigh, its tail swinging between his knees.

"Let go, lizard!"

"He's an iguana, not a lizard," I pointed out, trying not to laugh too hard.

"He's biting me through my pants! I'm going to die!"

"You're not going to die. Iguanas don't have venom. You would know that, Joe, if you had done your research before the mission."

"Spare me the lecture, professor. Just tell me how to *get him off of me!*"

Joe started spinning in circles, which only made the iguana clamp down harder.

"Stop moving, Joe!" I shouted. "You need to relax. Both you *and* the iguana need to relax . . . or he'll never unhinge his jaw."

"*Now* you tell me."

Joe stopped spinning and sat down on the curb. The iguana wriggled a few times between his legs, then finally began to lie still. Joe exhaled. The little green critter looked up at him with round, unblinking eyes.

"I think he likes you," I said.

"I think you shouldn't crack jokes while your only brother is trapped in the jaws of death."

Just then, the iguana opened its mouth—and let go of Joe's leg.

"Ah . . . relief!"

With a sigh, Joe started rubbing the bite mark on his leg through a hole in his torn pants.

"Look! Here come the police!" I said, nodding at a pair of approaching squad cars.

"In the nick of time," Joe grumbled. "They can lock up this green menace to society before he does any more damage."

The iguana gazed up at Joe and blinked.

"Don't look at me like that."

Believe it or not, I think my brother was starting to *like* the little guy.

Until the iguana was startled by the police siren. And took another bite of Joe's leg.

Twenty minutes later everything seemed to be under control.

A local team of wildlife experts returned all the animals to their cages—and removed the iguana from Joe's thigh. All it took was a drop of alcohol, and the creature released its grip quickly and quietly.

Joe, however, was a different story. He howled in pain until someone administered a Band-Aid.

"Be brave, Joe," I teased.

My brother shot me a dirty look. "What about Outback Mack?" he asked. "Did he get away?"

"The police took him to the hospital. It seems he wrecked his van a few miles down the road."

"He wrecked his van?"

"Yeah. He drove too fast over a speed bump and busted open a box full of rain forest spiders inside the van."

Joe laughed and shook his head. "Serves him right."

"So where's your little friend?" I asked.

Joe shrugged and adjusted his Band-Aid. "I guess he crawled off for an after-dinner nap."

"Poor little baby."

"Hey, that poor little baby bit me."

"I was talking about you."

The police thanked us for the evidence we dug up on Outback Mack's illegal animal trading. One of the wildlife experts waved to us from the entrance to the warehouse.

"Does this belong to you boys?" He held something up.

Joe's CD player.

"Yeah, that's mine," said Joe, running up to retrieve his player and earphones.

"Did you have any problem getting the king cobra back into his cage?" I asked.

The man shrugged. "Not really. He was just lying there, grooving to the music you left him. The only problem I had was prying the player out of his jaws."

"No kidding," said Joe, pointing to the two big fang holes in the plastic casing.

"Man, he really sank his teeth into it," I said.

Joe slapped me on the back. "Like I said, the new Thrasher CD totally rocks."

Hopping on our motorcycles, we headed home to Bayport. Joe listened to his CD player for the entire ride. I was amazed that the thing still worked.

"Put that away," I said as we pulled our motorcycles behind Aunt Trudy's Volkswagen.

Joe ignored me. He just kept bobbing his head to the music. I knew he had it on low volume for safety—but he acted as if it was on full blast.

"Joe." I grabbed him by the arm and plucked the earphones from his ears.

"What?"

"Hide your CD player," I said. "I don't want to have to explain the snake bites to Mom and Aunt Trudy."

They didn't know that Joe and I were undercover agents for ATAC. I hated lying to them, but our dad, a former cop, thought it would be safer for everyone to keep our missions a secret.

Joe stuffed the player into his leather jacket pocket and let out a little groan. "Now I'll have to listen to *their* music." He nodded toward the house.

A Big Band melody echoed throughout the old Victorian, and a velvety voice crooned corny lyrics from days gone by.

"Dad must have bought the Frank Sinatra collection on CD," I pointed out.

"Great." Joe crossed the porch and pushed open the front door. "Do you kids have to play your music so loud?" he shouted. "You're going to burst your eardrums!"

Mom and Dad stood in the middle of the living room with startled looks on their faces—and their arms around each other.

"Aha!" I said. "Caught you dancing! I always wondered what you two did when we weren't around."

"I blame it on Sinatra," Joe teased. "His music is corrupting yesterday's youth. It leads to jitterbugging."

"Actually, we were doing the foxtrot," Dad explained.

"Even worse," said Joe with a grin. "I just don't

understand how you can listen to all that old stuff. It's so not cool."

Mom rolled her eyes. "And I suppose *your* music is cool," she said. "What's that new band you like? Trashbag?"

"Thrasher."

"Whatever. It sounds like a trash compactor with a rhythm section. How can you prefer *that* to the timeless classics of Frank Sinatra? And what on earth happened to your pants?"

Oops.

I'd made Joe hide his snake-bitten CD player, but I'd forgotten all about his iguana-ripped pants.

"Oh, this?" said Joe. "Just a little accident."

"A *motorcycle* accident?" Mom gasped. "I knew it. Those bikes are just too dangerous for—"

"It wasn't a motorcycle accident, Mom," I interrupted. "We were playing touch football after school and it, um, turned into tackle football."

She shook her head. "You boys should be more careful."

If she only knew.

"Well, wash up for dinner. Aunt Trudy's making pot roast tonight."

Joe and I dropped our backpacks on the dining room table just as Aunt Trudy burst through the kitchen door.

"Freeze!" she snapped. "What did I tell you boys about dumping your backpacks on the dining room table?"

"Don't do it," I answered.

"That's right," she said. "I'm ready to set the table and the last thing I want to do is—AAAAUU-UUGHHH!"

Her scream made us all jump.

"What's wrong?" asked Dad, running into the room.

Aunt Trudy pointed a long finger at Joe's backpack. "It moved! I swear his backpack moved! There's something in there! Something alive!"

I glanced nervously at Joe.

Something must have escaped from Outback Mack's Animal Shack.

3.

Surprise Packages

I had no idea *what* could be wriggling and squirm-
ing inside my backpack. But *man,* I hoped it wasn't
anything poisonous.

"Everybody stand back," said Frank. "Something
must've crawled in there while we were, uh, playing football in the park."

"Oh, my!" said Aunt Trudy. "Do you think it's a
squirrel? Or a rat? Please say no."

"I don't think it's a squirrel *or* a rat," I muttered
under my breath. "But don't worry. I'll take care of
it . . . whatever it is."

Please don't be a snake. . . . Please don't be a snake. . . .

I leaned over the table and carefully unzipped
the wriggling backpack.

"Easy," I whispered.

Everybody jumped when the backpack flopped onto its side—and something crawled out.

Something green and scaly.

"Joe! It's your buddy!" Frank said, laughing.

The baby iguana took a few steps and stopped in the middle of the table, staring at us.

"A *lizard*?" Aunt Trudy shrieked. "How did a lizard get into your backpack?"

"I saw him in the pet store downtown," I lied, thinking fast. "And he's not a lizard. He's an iguana."

Aunt Trudy made a face. "I don't care what it is," she said. "I won't have it sitting on my dining room table. It'll ruin my appetite."

A tiny tongue darted in and out of the iguana's mouth—and Aunt Trudy screamed.

"Get rid of that thing right now!" she wailed. "And don't even *think* about adopting it. That parrot of yours, Playback, is bad enough, squawking and pooping all over the house. The last thing I need is a big lizard to clean up after. This isn't the Bayport Zoo."

Unfortunately for us, today clearly wasn't one of Aunt Trudy's "I love the parrot!" days. Sometimes she liked him, and sometimes she *really* didn't.

"We can't just throw him outside, Aunt Trudy," said Frank. "He won't survive in the cold."

Aunt Trudy stared at the baby iguana—which

stared right back at her. She sighed. "Oh, all right. He can spend the night here. But he has to go back to the pet store. First thing tomorrow, got it?"

"Got it," I said. "Thanks, Aunt Trudy."

"Come on, Joe," said Frank, slapping my arm. "Let's find a box for him in the garage."

We turned and walked out of the house, leaving Aunt Trudy alone with the iguana. Walking across the yard, Frank nudged me and shook his head.

"Man, that was close," he said. "We're lucky it was the iguana and not a cobra in your backpack."

"No problem, dude. We could've lulled the cobra to sleep with Frank Sinatra music."

Frank laughed.

I glanced up and squinted my eyes. *What's that?*

Something floated down from the sky, right over our heads.

"Check it out, Frank."

A tiny parachute descended slowly to the lawn, landing in a patch of Aunt Trudy's prize tomatoes. A small brown package was tied to the parachute's strings.

Frank reached down and picked it up. "Looks like ATAC sent us another mission, Joe." He squinted at the sky, probably trying to figure out how it was dropped. Thing is, it's hard to figure out ATAC messenger methods.

"Man, we just finished a mission," I groaned. "When am I going to do my homework?"

Just then Dad opened the living room window and shouted out to me. "Joe! Could you come inside? Your mother and I would like to have a talk with you."

"Sure, Dad. What's up?"

"Not your grades."

Oh, no. Not now.

My stomach flipped a few times. Dad closed the window, and I glanced at Frank.

"They must have seen my report card," I explained.

Frank gave me a sympathetic look. "Sorry, man," he said, patting my shoulder. "But you're on your own. I'll sneak the mission package upstairs inside the box for the iguana. Good luck."

He turned and headed for the garage while I went inside to face the firing squad.

What am I going to tell them? That it's hard to write book reports while I'm fighting off killer cobras?

Mom and Dad were waiting for me in the living room. They sat side by side on the sofa, gazing down at my report card on the coffee table.

Exhibit A.

I had received all Bs this semester—and a C in computer class.

Guilty, your honor.

I sat down in the armchair next to the fireplace and awaited my sentence.

"I'm not going to lecture you, Joe," my father started off. "But your grades seem to be slipping every semester. You used to be a straight A student."

I stared down at the floor, not knowing what to say.

Mom leaned forward. "Honey, I know you've been busy with all your extracurricular activities," she said. "But maybe you've taken on too much. You've never gotten a C before."

Dad shook his head. "Do you know what a C means, Joe? It means average. And I *know* you're not average. I *know* you can do better."

I sighed. *How can I tell them that Mr. Conner just doesn't seem to like me? It'll sound like an excuse.*

"Well, I guess I never bothered to focus on computers because Frank always took care of it here at home," I explained. "He's the computer whiz of the family."

Dad nodded. "Maybe you should ask him to help you."

I looked up at my father. "You know I hate to ask anyone for help. Especially Frank. He'll just tease me."

23

"No, he won't," he said. "Why do you think I give you boys so much freedom? Because I know you'll help each other out. No matter what."

I thought about it. Maybe Dad was right. Frank would definitely help me with my computer class—but I guess I was too proud to ask.

"Okay," I said. "I'll talk to him about it."

"Good," my father replied. "You can go now."

"Really? No punishment?"

"Do you want one?"

"No."

"Then get out of here."

I dashed upstairs and headed for Frank's room. And that's when I heard the screams.

"Burned! Burned! Burned!"

I opened the door. Frank was sitting at his desk in front of the computer while our pet parrot, Playback, flew in circles over his head.

"Burned!"

"That's right, Playback," Frank cooed to the bird. "That's the name of our new mission."

"Burned!"

Playback squawked and flapped, then perched on top of the computer monitor.

"Burned?" I said, pulling up a chair. "Are we hunting down arsonists?"

Frank shrugged. "Guess we'll find out." He took

24

a CD from the mission box and popped it into his computer.

I reached for the box. "What else is in here?"

"Just pay attention."

The computer screen went black, and an explosion of sound burst through the speakers. First there was a cymbal crash, then a symphony orchestra, followed by a jazz band, a gospel choir, and a 1950s doo-wop group. Seconds later a heavy pounding beat turned it all into one big disco anthem—which somehow morphed into a wacky rock/rap/hip-hop symphony.

"And I thought Frank Sinatra was bad," I commented.

White lines streaked across the black screen, forming long columns of sheet music. Colored notes danced across the lines in rhythm with the mishmash of melodies.

"Welcome to the wonderful world of music," a voice boomed through the speakers. I wondered who it was. Usually it was the voice of Q.T., head of ATAC, but not always. *"For decades people have enjoyed many styles of music. But there was only one way to buy music: on vinyl LP records from the local music store."*

The colored notes swirled in a circle and formed a round black record album with a blue label in the center.

"In the 1960s and '70s, music became available in a

variety of other formats, including reel-to-reel tapes, eight-track cartridges, and cassette tapes."

On the screen the round black record morphed from one format to the other as the narrator spoke.

"Then, in the 1980s, computers changed everything. Music went digital, and albums were downloaded onto durable compact discs."

The tapes on the screen turned into a single shiny CD. The background pulsed with electronic graphics, forming a web of interlocking lines.

"The growth of personal computers and the Internet brought this new digital technology into homes all over the world. By the 1990s people could download perfect copies of their favorite songs and albums directly from the World Wide Web. And that's where the problems began."

The picture of the CD froze on the screen—and a wall of prison bars slammed down over the image.

"Illegal downloads became a common criminal activity. Record companies lost millions of dollars. Musicians and songwriters lost control of their copyrights. And the biggest culprits of this new techno-crime were . . . teenage music fans."

A pair of eyes appeared on the CD, then a nose, mouth, and baseball cap.

"Recently the government has cracked down on Web sites offering illegal downloads to consumers. The problem still exists, but it's basically under control. *Each download, however—even if it's purchased legally—can be used to create a perfect copy of the original music. Some people have begun to mass-produce downloaded albums, burning them onto homemade CDs for resale on the underground market. This is highly illegal. Which brings us to Bayport High School.*"

I glanced at Frank. "Bayport High School?"

A picture of our school appeared on the screen, and the narrator continued. "*A nationwide distribution of illegal CDs has been traced to your hometown school. And we have reason to believe one of your classmates may be involved.*"

A face appeared on the screen.

"I know him," I said. "He's in my gym class."

"*His name is Julian Sanders,*" the voice explained. "*Although we don't believe he's the mastermind behind it, we suspect he burns illegal copies for a major crime ring, which then sells the CDs to foreign countries.*"

"That would explain the classic Corvette he drives," I mumbled.

Frank shushed me as the narrator continued.

"*Your mission, boys, is to gather hard evidence of Julian's involvement and—if you can—uncover his higher-level contacts. We've included a few new toys in the mission box that might come in handy. And remember: This mission, like every mission, is top secret. In five*

27

seconds this disk will be reformatted into a standard music CD."

Five, four, three, two, one . . .

The image disappeared from the screen, and a singer's voice crooned through the speakers.

Frank Sinatra.

I groaned and reached over to change the CD. Removing the reformatted disc, I handed it to Playback, who snapped it up in his beak and flew across the room.

"Enough of that garbage," I said. "Let's listen to some *real* music." I pulled my CD player from my jacket, opened it, and took out the CD with "Thrasher" written on it in Magic Marker.

"Where did you get that, Joe?" Frank asked, standing over me.

"This? Chet Morton made a copy for me."

Frank opened the top drawer of his dresser, reached inside, and turned back to face me. He held something in his hands.

A pair of handcuffs.

Huh?

"I'm sorry, Joe," said my brother. "I'm going to have to place you under arrest."

He reached for my wrists.

Dude!

"You're kidding, right?"

"Does it look like I'm kidding?" He snapped a cuff around my left wrist.

And that's when I tackled him to the floor.

"You'll never take me alive!"

"Bring it on, bro!"

4.

Top 40 Suspects

Joe and I wrestled with the handcuffs—and laughed our heads off—until Aunt Trudy yelled at us to stop horsing around.

"Come and eat, boys! My pot roast is getting cold!"

"Okay, we're coming!" I shouted through the door.

Joe grabbed my arm as I started to go. "Wait, Frank. I have a couple of quick questions for you."

"Shoot."

He took a deep breath. "I got a C in my computer class. Partly because Mr. Conner doesn't like me. But mostly because I'm having trouble with his assignments." Joe lowered his head a bit, then

The e-mail contained an attachment. I clicked twice on it, and a few seconds later music played through my speakers.

It was a new dance mix of the song "Heart-breaker."

This reminded her of me? No way.

"What're you listening to, Frank?"

Joe walked into the room, smiling.

"Nothing," I said, turning off the monitor. "Let's check out our new stuff for the mission."

I opened the box while Joe stared at me suspiciously.

"Was that an e-mail from Belinda I saw on your computer?" he asked.

"Never mind. Look at this." I handed him a portable digital sound recorder with a wireless microphone that was smaller than a dime.

"Look. The microphone has a peel-and-stick tab."

"Yeah, so you can secretly attach it to someone and record their conversations," I said, glancing at the instructions. "It says here that this little recorder can pick up the microphone's signal almost a mile away."

"Wow. And what's this for?" Joe asked, pulling a soda can from the mission box. "In case we get thirsty?"

"No, it's a spy cam," I explained. "With night

vision. It can record an image in almost total darkness. And transmit it instantly to any computer using this receiver."

I held up another small device with a mini satellite dish. Joe nodded, then studied the soda can more carefully.

"Aha. Here's the camera lens hidden in the center."

He set the can down, pulled an envelope from the box, and whistled.

"Check out all the cash, Frank! Man, we could have a lot of fun with this!"

I snatched the money away from him. "Chill, Joe. I think we're supposed to use it to buy illegal CDs as evidence."

Joe frowned. "You take the fun out of everything . . . you *heartbreaker.*"

I growled and tackled him to the floor.

The next morning we prepared for Day One of our new mission—and for another day of school. I reluctantly unlocked the handcuffs from Joe's wrist and slipped the digital sound recorder into my jacket. I planned to take notes on *everybody*— even our friend Chet Morton, who'd burned the Thrasher CD for Joe.

"Don't forget to return that lizard creature to the

pet store!" Aunt Trudy shouted to us as we headed out the door.

"We'll try to do it after school," I told her.

"Try hard," she insisted.

As we revved up our motorcycles, Joe gave me a look. "You know we don't have time to drive the iguana all the way back to Outback Mack's. What are we going to do with him?"

I shrugged. "Maybe Chet will take him in."

"Chet? He's not crazy about responsibility for animals."

"How does he feel about going to jail for illegal CD burning?" I asked.

"I think he'd rather have a pet iguana."

Minutes later we pulled our motorcycles into the school parking lot. As soon as we turned off the engines, a large SUV zoomed up next to us and screeched to halt. Loud throbbing music pounded through the windows.

"Yo! Hardys! Check out my new speakers!"

It was Brian Conrad, the biggest butthead of Bayport High. The guy was a bully, a jerk, a thug, and a creep—and those were his good qualities.

"I've been burning a whole slew of CDs, too," he bragged. "Punk, rap, hip-hop, metal, even some top forty garbage . . . for my sister here."

He rolled his eyes, nodding toward the passenger seat.

Belinda waved and hopped out of the van.

"Hi, Frank." She smiled and ran a hand through her long blond hair. "Did you get my e-mail?"

Gulp.

I could feel my face turning red.

"Yeah, he got it," Joe blurted out. "What's up with that song you sent him? You think my brother here is a heartbreaker?"

Now Belinda's face started to turn red.

I smacked Joe in the stomach. "Come on. We're going to be late."

Pulling the digital recorder from my jacket, I lowered my voice and made a quick note: "Tuesday, 7:55 a.m. Bayport student Brian Conrad admits to burning CDs. Accompanied by his sister, Belinda, who sent me a downloaded song via e-mail yesterday. Both must be considered suspects."

Joe stared at me and shook his head. "You better take it easy, Sherlock. Take a look around. *Everybody* burns their own CDs."

I glanced down the row of lockers. Just a few feet away some students were shoving earphones into their ears—and homemade discs into their CD players.

"Do you plan to put the entire school behind bars?" Joe asked me.

Turns out he had a point.

Through the course of three morning classes, I witnessed a shocking amount of suspicious behavior. Here's just a small sampling of what I recorded:

"Tuesday, 8:05 a.m. Three Bayport juniors exchange unlabeled CDs outside the science lab. Suspects include Melinda Metz, Clarissa Tartar, and Maggie McMahon."

"Tuesday, 9:16 a.m. Sophomore Steve Rubin hands an unidentified amount of cash to senior Ralph Balass in front of the Pep Squad booth in the school lobby. In return, Ralph gives Steve two unmarked CD jewel cases."

"Tuesday, 9:58 a.m. Freshman Jean Martinet sits in study hall with a CD player on her desk. It's hooked up to a mini digital music player on her lap. Illegal downloading suspected."

Joe was right after all.

In fact, I had managed to put together a list of

forty suspects—and it wasn't even lunchtime yet.

Man! Forty suspects!

"Hi there, Frank!"

I looked up to see our friend Chet Morton walking toward me down the hall.

Make that forty-one.

"Hi, Chet."

My brother was right behind him. "Guess what, Frank? Chet said he'd care take of the iguana for us. Isn't that great?"

"Yeah, great," I said. "Thanks, Chet."

Chet shrugged and grinned. "Iguanas are cool. I have an old aquarium in the basement. I can fix it up real nice for the little guy."

I nodded. "Look, Chet. I wanted to ask you about that Thrasher CD you made for Joe."

Chet stopped me. "Don't worry, it's legal. I paid for the download on the Internet."

"Yeah, but aren't you supposed to use it on your digital player? I don't know if you're allowed to make a hard copy of it on CD."

Chet scratched his head. "Gee, I'm not sure."

"I'll ask Mr. Conner about it," I said. "The guy knows everything about computers. Maybe he's up on Internet copyright law, too."

"Well, get back to me on that," said Chet. "If I'm

doing something illegal, I'd like to know about it. Later, dudes."

Sticking a pair of earphones in his ears, he turned and walked off.

Joe grabbed my arm and led me toward the drinking fountain. "Listen. I have gym class next period with Julian Sanders," he whispered. "I'll try to get him talking about what kind of music he likes, then ask him if he'll make me some CDs of his favorite groups."

I looked my brother in the eye. "Be careful, Joe."

He rolled his eyes. "Oh, please. What's he going to do? Kill me over a bunch of songs?"

5.
Dodging Questions

Be careful? Me?

I didn't know what Frank was so worried about. But then again, we *did* almost get killed on our last mission.

Remember the king cobra?

I shook off the memory and headed for the boys' locker room. Pushing open the door, I walked slowly past the first few rows of lockers.

Okay, Julian Sanders. Where are you hiding?

Finally I spotted him in the corner, away from the other boys. Hoisting my gym bag over my shoulders, I grabbed a locker near his and started to undress.

"Hi, Julian."

He glared at me through a mop of black hair that

covered half his face. He was wearing a concert T-shirt for Sinkhole, a band I'd never heard of, and a pair of faded jeans he'd doodled on with a ballpoint pen.

"Aren't you Joe Hardy?" he asked suspiciously.

"Yeah."

"Don't you usually grab a locker next to all the jocks over there?"

I glanced at my friends across the locker room, then looked back at Julian. "They've been working my nerves lately," I said in a low voice. "We hung out together all weekend, and man, if I hear any more of that jock rock they listen to, I think I might barf."

Julian tilted his head, a lock of hair falling over his eyes. "Oh, yeah? What kind of music do you like?"

Yes! It's working!

I pulled my gym shirt over my head and shrugged. "I don't know. I guess I'm into the new underground stuff. You know, groups like Skunkcabbage, the Blisters, Bad Breath, and, oh yeah, Pushing Up Daisies. I really dig them."

Julian nodded slowly, obviously impressed with my taste in music.

"Have you heard of the Stale Cupcakes?" he asked me.

41

"Dude! They're awesome! Those girls totally kick butt! Their guitar solos slay me!"

Julian smiled—in spite of the too-cool-for-school attitude he wore like a permanent Halloween mask.

I'm in. He likes me.

"You surprise me," he said. "I mean, I never thought clean-cut Joe Hardy would know about the Cupcakes, let alone like them."

"Are you kidding? I'm always on the lookout for new bands."

"Yeah?"

Here's my chance.

I sat next to Julian and pulled on my sneakers. "Do you think you could hook me up with some new stuff?" I asked. "You know. Stuff I won't find at the megastore. Something radical."

Julian stared at me thoughtfully, but he didn't answer my question.

"I'm sick of all the Top Forty clones on the radio," I added. "You got to help me out, man."

Julian pulled up his gym trunks and sighed. "I guess I could write down the names of some bands for you."

"That'd be cool," I said. "But it'd be even cooler if you could make some CDs for me."

Oops. I think I spoke too soon.

Julian turned away from me and slammed his locker.

"Making copies is illegal, man," he said under his breath.

"What's the big deal, dude?" I urged. "You must have hundreds of CDs at home."

"Yeah, so?"

"I'd give anything to have a collection half as good as yours," I went on. "But I just can't afford to buy new CDs right now. I've already spent most of the money I made last summer. And my family's not rich. My dad retired last year."

Julian shook the hair off his face and looked at me. "Wasn't your dad a cop?"

"So? Do you think I'd tell him about it?"

"Probably not. But what if he finds them?"

"I doubt if he'd send his own son to the slammer."

"Really?" said Julian. "I heard you Hardys are total Boy Scouts."

"Not when it comes to music."

Julian shook his head. "I don't know, man. Your dad's a cop."

"He's retired."

"It's too risky."

"Aw, come on."

Julian laced up his sneakers and started heading out to the gym.

"Julian, wait," I said, running after him. "I'm willing to pay you."

He stopped in his tracks.

That got him.

"Name your price," I continued. "Whatever you want, so long as it's cheaper than paying full price."

Slowly he turned around to face me.

I got him on the hook now. All I have to do is reel him in.

There was just one problem.

The expression on Julian's face had completely changed. In fact, he looked kind of angry.

Like the king cobra.

And I had to jump back when he suddenly lashed out at me.

"Just drop it, Hardy!"

Julian's voice echoed across the gymnasium. All the other guys in our class stopped talking to see what was going on.

"I don't get you," he snarled at me. "First you act like I don't exist all semester, then *wham*. You turn on the Mister Nice Guy act so you can weasel something out of me."

"Julian, no, I just—"

"You just what? Want to get me in trouble? Is that it?"

"No, man, I—"

"Don't waste your breath, *dude*. I don't know what your game is, but I'm not playing. Got it?"

He started walking away.

"Julian . . ."

"I'm warning you, Hardy!" he yelled over his shoulder. "DROP IT!"

There was a moment of silence in the gym. Then all my friends started hooting.

"Are you going take that, Joe?"

"Yeah! Go kick his butt!"

"You can take him, Joe!"

I was about to tell them all to shut up when Mr. Mirabella, the gym teacher, did it for me.

"Knock it off, boys!" he shouted. "Let's see you channel that energy into a healthy game of dodgeball! Come on, guys, move it!"

A few of the boys ran to the storage room to get the balls.

"Hardy! Sanders! You're team leaders!" Mr. Mirabella bellowed. "Start choosing sides! Let's go!"

I glanced at Julian across the court. He glared back at me with a wicked sneer.

"You're going down, Hardy!" he growled.

Then he picked the biggest, meanest guy in class for his team.

Back and forth, we chose sides until two teams faced each other from opposite sides of the court.

Someone had tossed Julian one of the balls, and he kept slamming it from one hand to the other and shooting me dirty looks.

"Okay, line up the balls on the center line," Mr. Mirabella ordered. "Then take your places on the back wall and wait for the whistle."

Everyone got into position.

I have to admit, my heart was pounding. Julian looked like he wanted to kill me.

What's up with that?

"Wait for the whistle," said Mr. Mirabella.

He clenched the silver whistle in his teeth, paused for a few seconds, then blew it.

Both teams rushed toward the row of balls on the center line. Julian was charging straight for the same ball I was heading for.

I reached down to grab the ball. But Julian beat me to it.

Screeching to a halt, I started running backward as fast as I could—while Julian fixed his eyes on me and took aim.

Easy, dude.

I couldn't believe the look on his face.

Or how hard he threw the ball.

Ouch! I staggered back, gasping. The dodge ball had slammed right into my gut.

And knocked me to the ground.

SUSPECT PROFILE

Name: Julian Thomas Sanders

Hometown: Bayport

Physical description: Sixteen years old, 5'11", 160 lbs., medium build, black hair, green eyes, silver ring in eyebrow, "alternative" dresser.

Occupation: Bayport High School student

Background: Mother divorced. Repeated third grade.

Suspicious behavior: Acted nervous when questioned about copying CDs, threw dodge ball as if it were a weapon.

Suspected of: Burning CDs for illegal distribution.

Possible motives: Easy money.

Believe it or not, I caught Julian's ball.

Which meant he had to sit on the sidelines until one of his players caught a ball and called him back into the game.

"Good catch, Hardy!" shouted Mr. Mirabella.

Maybe it *was* a good catch. But my stomach didn't think so. The force of Julian's throw really packed a wallop. I was afraid I was going to throw up.

But then I had something else to worry about.

Julian was coaching his whole team to go after me.

"Get him, guys!" he yelled. "Get Hardy!"

Before I could even regain my footing, a whole swarm of dodge balls came flying toward me. I tried to jump and turn, but . . .

WHAM.

Four or five balls hit me all at once, knocking me over like a human bowling pin.

Ooof.

I landed with a heavy thud on the gymnasium floor.

"Hardy! You're out!" the gym teacher shouted.

As if I didn't know that.

I staggered to my feet and limped to the sideline. Taking a deep breath, I glanced up to see Julian laughing at me.

"I'm not through with you yet, Hardy," he said.

And he wasn't lying.

Soon both of us were called back into the game by our teammates. I managed to knock him out again with a direct hit, but as soon as one of his players caught a ball, he was back in the game. And out to get me.

WHAM.

He hit me hard in the knee.

POW.

I returned the favor as soon as I got back in the game.

SMACK.

He got me again.

And so on and so forth, round after round, until Mr. Mirabella blew the final whistle.

"Okay, boys! That's enough! Hit the showers! And don't forget to put the dodge balls away!"

The gym teacher disappeared into his office while I grabbed a couple of balls and headed for the storage room. I could hear someone running after me.

"Hardy! Wait!"

I turned around to see Julian running straight toward me. He wiped sweat from his forehead with one hand—and hurled a dodge ball with the other.

"Dodge *this*!"

The ball came flying at me so fast I could barely see it. I tried to duck, but it was too late.

BANG.

The ball hit me square in the face.

And knocked me unconscious.

6.

The Web of Crime

I was on my way to the computer room when Chet told me the news.

"Joe is in the nurse's office."

What did my brother do now? Challenge Julian to a duel?

"Julian Sanders hit Joe in the face with a dodge ball," Chet explained. "He was knocked out cold."

"Is he all right?" I asked, gazing down the hall toward the nurse's office.

"Yeah, he's fine. Nurse Jones made him lie down and rest for a while. He said he felt fine and tried to put up a fight but she insisted."

Yep, that sounds like Joe.

"Maybe I should go see if he's okay," I said, pushing past Chet. "Go to the computer room and tell Mr. Conner I had to cancel our appointment."

"Frank! Wait!"

Chet grabbed me by the arm.

"Nurse Jones won't let anybody see him right now. She said they'd have to get past her first."

Yep, that sounds like Nurse Jones.

"Okay. If that's the case, I might as well keep my appointment with Mr. Conner."

I turned around and pushed past Chet—again.

And Chet tried to stop me—again.

"Frank! Wait!"

I spun around. "Now what, Chet?"

"Are you going to talk to Mr. Conner about— you know—downloading music from the Internet and burning CDs?"

"Yeah."

"Do me a favor." He lowered his voice. "Don't mention my name, okay? I don't want to get in any trouble."

"Sure. I got you covered. Later, Chet."

I headed for the computer room, still a little worried about my brother.

What am I worried about? Joe can handle anything. Cobras, iguanas, dodge balls. He'll be fine.

I knocked lightly on the door to the computer room.

"Come in."

I went inside. "Hi, Mr. Conner. Thanks for seeing me."

Mr. Conner sat at his desk in front of a computer keyboard and screen. He looked sort of like a hippie from the 1960s, with a woolly beard, little round glasses, and long graying hair tied in a ponytail. He always wore a tie and a suit that was two sizes too big for his tall, thin frame.

I guess he wore the suit to look more professional. Otherwise he'd look like a roadie for a rock band.

"Hi, Frank. What do you want to talk to me about?"

He offered me a chair. I sat down and made up a story.

"I'm writing a story for my journalism class about downloading music from the Internet. Do you know anything about that?"

Mr. Conner leaned back in his chair. "Well, the laws differ from country to country, but I know a little bit about it. What do you want to know?"

I reached into my pocket and pulled out a notepad and pen. "Let's see. I've noticed kids here at school sharing copies of music CDs. Is that legal?"

The computer teacher leaned forward and stroked his beard thoughtfully. "Well, it depends. You're allowed to download music from a Web site directly onto your own computer or digital music player, as long as you've paid for it. But it's illegal to share that file with someone who *hasn't* paid for it. That's breaking copyright laws."

"I see warnings about copyright on CDs and DVDs and stuff all the time, but I'm not exactly sure what it is."

"It's legal ownership of creative property. Every songwriter has a copyright on the music he or she writes. Just like authors have copyrights for their books."

I jotted down some notes and asked another question. "If you paid for the music download from a Web site, then can you burn it onto a CD?"

Mr. Conner raised an eyebrow. "It's iffy," he said. "Typically, you're permitted to burn one legal download onto a CD if it's for your personal use only. But if you burn a CD for a friend, then it's illegal. The other person hasn't paid for the copyright."

I shook my head. "I think a lot of students are breaking the law and don't even realize it."

"You're probably right," he agreed.

"Here's another question," I continued. "What about the other way around? What if I bought a CD in a store and my friend copied it onto his digital player?"

"That's also illegal."

"Wow, those are pretty tough laws."

"They were created to protect the copyrights, Frank," Mr. Conner explained. "Think about it. A lot of people put a lot of work into every song you hear. Musicians, singers, engineers, production crews, record companies. Only a small handful of them get rich, mostly through tours and shows. Most recording artists don't profit much from their albums. They get only a tiny percentage of every copy sold."

"I never thought of it that way."

"And besides, stealing is wrong. That's what you're doing when you copy a friend's CD. You're stealing."

I stopped taking notes and gazed around the room. There were rows and rows of desks, each with its own computer terminal. On top of a file cabinet sat a stack of CD cases.

"Are those blank CDs over there?"

Mr. Conner turned and looked. "Yes. As you know, all students back up their work onto discs. If they didn't, the hard drives of all these computers would be stuffed full."

I surveyed the classroom.

"All of these are equipped with CD burners?"

Mr. Conner nodded. "I had to beg the school to

get them. The old machines were so outdated they were useless."

I stared at the computers and started thinking.

Anyone in the school can come in here and burn illegal CDs.

"You must go through a lot of blank CDs," I said.

"Thousands."

"Where do you keep them all?"

Mr. Conner seemed a little confused by my question. "I keep the supplies in the storage room. Back there."

He pointed to a door in the corner.

"Could I take a look?"

He shrugged. "Sure. Why not? Though I don't understand how it'll help you write a story about music copyright theft."

"I'm just curious."

He opened the top drawer of his desk and pulled out a large ring of keys.

"You keep it locked?" I asked.

"Of course," he said, standing up. "I store some valuable equipment back there . . . and thousands of dollars' worth of blank CDs, software programs, and supplies."

Mr. Conner walked to the corner and fidgeted with the keys.

"Are those the only keys to the room?" I asked him.

He stopped and looked at me.

"Well, no. There are spare keys in the main office. And the janitors have a set too. Some of the other teachers use this classroom, so I suppose they might have keys as well. Why do you ask?"

I didn't know what to say. Why *would* I ask him about his keys?

Because I'm an undercover agent for American Teens Against Crime?

No, I had to think of something.

"Sorry to be so nosy, Mr. Conner. I'm writing another article on the subject of school security. I figured I could kill two birds with one stone."

The teacher turned around slowly and pointed a finger at me.

"Very clever, Frank," he said. "You always were one of my best students."

"Thanks, Mr. Conner."

He turned back to the lock, found the right key, and opened the door. "Here we go," he said, flicking on a light. "Come take a look."

I followed him into the small room—and almost bashed right into him.

"I don't believe this!" he said, gasping.

"Believe what? What's wrong?"

I glanced around at the steel shelves lining the room. Everything seemed normal—cardboard boxes stacked up on one side and a few dusty computers on the other.

Mr. Conner shook his head. "It looks like you've found your story, Frank."

"What?"

"Your article about school security."

He pointed at the empty shelves.

"What are you talking about, Mr. Conner?"

"They were here yesterday, but it looks like someone stole them. Every last one of them."

"Stole what?"

"Twenty cases of blank CDs."

7.

Money to Burn

Nurse Jones is trying to kill me.

That was the only explanation for all the cold compresses the school nurse piled onto my face and head. I swear the woman was trying to smother me to death.

"I can't breathe," I tried to tell her.

But my words were garbled, swallowed up by the wet towels.

Finally, after about two hours, she told me to sit up. "I think you'll be all right, Joe."

No kidding. I was hit by a dodge ball, not a school bus.

Pulling the compresses off my face, Nurse Jones examined me through her giant thick glasses.

"The redness is gone," she observed. "You're lucky your nose wasn't broken."

"I'll feel lucky as soon as you let me out of here," I said. "Can I leave now? I feel perfectly fine."

She nodded reluctantly. I swung my legs over the side of the examination table and hopped off.

"Are you experiencing any headache or pain?" she asked for the millionth time.

"No, but *you* will if you don't stop asking me that."

Nurse Jones smirked. "Okay, wise guy. Get out of here. And be careful!"

Everybody keeps saying that to me. But do I listen?

"Oh, I forgot to tell you, Joe. Someone's waiting for you outside," she added. "And he seems very concerned about you."

It must be Frank. Who else worries so much?

"Thanks, Nurse Jones," I said, turning and opening the door to her office.

I started thinking of something funny to say to Frank—and then I got the surprise of a lifetime.

Frank wasn't waiting for me outside the office. It was Julian Sanders.

"Julian?"

He pushed a lock of black hair away from his eyes—and revealed a face racked with guilt. "Look, Joe. I feel awful about all this. I don't know why I got so mad. I guess I'm not used to one of the 'in' crowd being nice to me."

Suddenly I felt a little guilty myself. After all, I was trying to gather criminal evidence from the guy.

"It's okay, Julian. If it makes you feel better, you didn't hurt me with the dodge ball. Actually, it hurt me more when you said that I've ignored you all semester—and you're right."

Julian didn't respond.

"Look, I think you're cool," I continued. "I should have talked to you long ago."

Julian sighed. "Thanks, man. What do you say I make it up to you? Come over to my house after school, take a look at my music collection, and I'll burn a mixed CD for you. No charge. Deal?"

"Deal."

We shook hands and parted ways.

Minutes later the afternoon bell rang and Frank spotted me across the hall.

"Joe! Wait till you hear this!"

He told me about his talk with Mr. Conner and the missing blank CDs.

"Well, wait till you hear *this,*" I said when Frank finished his story.

I told him about Julian's surprise visit to the nurse's office and his offer to show me his music collection after school.

"This is your chance, Joe. You've got to go with him and look around for evidence."

Frank pulled a tiny object from his shirt pocket.

"What's that?"

"The wireless microphone. Take it with you and I'll record everything. Just in case."

I took the microphone and slipped it into my jacket.

"And one more thing."

Here it comes.

"Be careful."

I met Julian in the lobby after school. He was waiting for me, leaning against the trophy case, bouncing his head to some music on his CD player.

He smiled when he spotted me.

"Hey, Joe. Ready to go?"

I couldn't help but feel a little nervous. I mean, this was the same guy who tried to remove my head with a dodge ball this morning.

Maybe it's a setup.

With a sinking feeling in my gut, I followed Julian out to the school parking lot. He led me straight to his car—a shiny red classic Corvette—and told me to hop in.

"I can follow you instead," I said, nodding toward my motorcycle.

61

Julian looked a little disappointed.

Why? Is he planning something?

"First check out this stereo system." Julian popped a disc into the car's player and pushed a button. The whole Corvette nearly exploded with the sound of hard punk music. "The Cupcakes. Listen to that bass!"

"Sweet."

While he revved up his engine, I walked back to my bike and whispered a quick message to my brother through the microphone in my pocket.

"All systems go, Frank. I'm following suspect Julian Sanders out of the parking lot."

Julian lived on the other side of town, on a dark narrow street of brown faded row houses. His bright red Corvette stuck out like a sore thumb in a neighborhood like this.

Pretty fancy car for a high school kid.

We parked right in front of Julian's house. The name Sanders was spelled out in stick-on letters on a rusty old mailbox.

I whispered the exact address into my microphone.

"Who are you talking to?"

"Oh, I'm just mumbling about my brakes. They're sticking a little."

"You should be careful."

Oh, no, not another warning.

Julian led me up the concrete steps to the front door. He didn't bother with keys. It was unlocked.

I hope he didn't bring me here to finish off what he started in gym class.

He held the door open for me. I half expected to be jumped by a couple of thugs as soon as I stepped inside. My heart was pounding.

And Julian's dodgeball threat echoed in my head. *You're going down, Hardy.*

It was dark inside, except for the blue light of an old TV set and the hot pink nightgown worn by his mother.

"Hi, baby," she said, not moving from the sofa. "Who's your friend?"

"Joe Hardy."

"Hardy? The policeman's son?"

"Yeah."

"Are we under arrest?"

"No, Mom. Go back to your game show."

Julian looked at me and rolled his eyes, then led me up a narrow flight of stairs to his bedroom.

"Wow. This is a cool room, Julian," I said.

And I meant it. The room was a cluttered mess, sure, but it was cluttered with very cool stuff: two state-of-the-art computers and flat screens, tons of stereo equipment, at least six massive speakers, shelves packed with CDs and record albums, and dozens of wild-looking concert posters.

"You haven't seen anything yet," Julian said with a sneaky grin.

He flicked a switch on the wall, and the whole room transformed into some sort of crazy nightclub. Disco balls and strobe lights flickered and whirled, blurring my vision and making me dizzy.

He's trying to blind me!

I braced myself for an attack. But then Julian snapped the club lights off and flopped down on his bed.

"Here. Check out these CDs. I think you'll like them."

I sat down and looked through his collection.

"Party Ghost, the Screaming Pickle, Greasy Kid Stuff, The Dog Ate My Homework . . . Man, I haven't heard of any of these bands," I said. "Are they any good?"

Julian smiled. "They're awesome. I'll pick out some of my favorites for you."

He grabbed a stack of CDs, crossed the room, and sat down at his computer. Flicking it on and inserting a blank CD, he went to work.

"Let me know if there's anything else there you want me to burn," he said.

I studied his gigantic collection of CDs. "Man, you have everything."

Julian nodded. "I downloaded most of them from the Internet. I know it's illegal to make copies for people—but you can't buy this stuff at the local Mega Mart."

So that makes it okay to rip off the musicians?

I didn't say anything.

"Considering all the CDs I buy, I figure the record company won't mind," he added. "They've got money to burn."

They're not the only ones.

I stared at Julian's sprawling assortment of electronic equipment. It must have cost him a fortune.

My eyes stopped at a large black notebook next to a pile of socks and T-shirts. It was opened to a page covered in writing and check marks.

One column was labeled "Blank CDs Received."

Another was labeled "Number of Copies."

The last column was labeled "Rate .50 Per Copy."

This is it. Hard evidence.

I glanced up at Julian. He was busy at his desk, downloading songs into a music file on his computer.

I looked down again at the notebook. Dozens of album titles were handwritten next to the columns.

Those are the albums he's burning.

Then I checked to see how many copies he was making of each.

500 copies. 1,000 copies. 2,500 copies.

I couldn't believe what I was seeing.

Julian Sanders is a one-man CD-burning factory!

"What are you looking at?"

I looked up to see Julian staring at me suspiciously.

"This Skunkcabbage album," I answered, pulling a CD from the shelf. "I've never seen it before. I thought I owned all of them."

With my left foot I closed the notebook on the floor.

"That's a bootleg from one of their concerts," said Julian, turning back to his computer.

I breathed a sigh of relief. Then I glanced back down at the notebook next to my foot. Something was written on the cover: "Jobs for C. D. Burns."

Who's C. D. Burns?

Then it hit me. C. D. Burns was the person who paid Julian to mass-produce CDs. He was the mastermind behind an illegal crime ring.

"All done."

Julian spun around in his chair and handed me the new mixed CD. He had even printed a label for it, listing all the songs and bands.

"Thanks, man. This is great."

Julian was about to say something—but then he spotted the notebook at my feet.

"Let me know what you think," he said, standing up. He reached down and picked up the notebook. "If you're into one of the band's songs, I can copy the whole album for you."

He opened a dresser drawer and slipped the notebook inside. For a split second, I thought I saw something else in the drawer.

A bunch of one-hundred-dollar bills.

Money to burn.

Julian turned around and looked me in the eye. "There's just one last thing, Joe."

I held my breath. "What?"

"Promise you'll never tell *anyone* about this."

I nodded and promised.

"I could get into a *lot* of trouble," he added. "*You* could get into a lot of trouble too."

Is that a threat?

"Don't worry about it, Julian," I said.

"I mean it, Joe. Seriously."

The look on his face made me nervous.

For the first time, Julian Sanders actually seemed scared.

8.

Mega Madness

"I wish you could have swiped Julian's notebook," I said to Joe. "Then we'd have our evidence."

My brother leaned back against a Team Spirit poster in the school hallway. "I don't know, Frank. I don't think Julian Sanders is the real villain here. He's working for C. D. Burns."

I glanced around to make sure none of the other students were listening. "Well, maybe the police should question Julian about C. D. Burns," I whispered.

"Julian wouldn't reveal his identity."

"How do you know?"

Joe looked me in the eye. "Because he's scared, Frank."

"He didn't sound scared on the recording."

"You didn't see his face."

"But Joe . . ."

I just couldn't convince him. For some reason, Joe didn't want to turn Julian in. Not yet, at least.

But the guy's guilty. We ought to tell the police.

The school bell brought an end to our discussion. Third period classes were starting, so Joe and I decided to talk about it later.

I walked down the hall toward the science lab. On the way I passed the empty computer room.

Maybe I should ask Mr. Conner what to do.

I stuck my head inside. "Mr. Conner?"

He looked up from his desk. There was someone next to him too.

Belinda Conrad.

The girl who thinks I'm a heartbreaker.

"I . . . I'm sorry to interrupt," I said, stammering. "I can come back another time."

Mr. Conner shook his head and waved me in. "Wait! Come in, Frank! I wanted to talk to you. Belinda and I are finished up here."

Belinda winked at me.

"Do you understand everything now, Belinda?" the teacher asked her.

"Yes, thank you, Mr. Conner," she said, brushing past me. "Hi, Frank. Bye, Frank."

Trying not to blush, I turned to Mr. Conner. He offered me a seat.

"I wanted to tell you what I learned about those stolen CDs," he said. "I informed Principal Foxworth about their disappearance, and guess what? It was all just a shipping error."

"A shipping error?"

"Yes. The computer supply company accidentally sent us a shipment that was supposed to go to Riverview High School. They came early yesterday morning to take them back. Our CD shipment will arrive on Monday."

That's bizarre.

"Why didn't they just send that shipment to Riverview and let Bayport keep the ones we got?"

Mr. Conner shrugged. "Who knows? Maybe they use a different brand than we do."

I wasn't buying it.

"Principal Foxworth told you this?"

The computer teacher nodded.

"Do you believe him?" I asked.

Mr. Conner started laughing. "Frank, I think you're trying too hard to come up with a good story for your journalism class. Shipping screwups happen all the time."

"I guess so," I said.

But I still didn't believe it.

Is Principal Foxworth in on the whole thing? Is he really C. D. Burns?

"What did you want to talk about, Frank?" Mr. Conner asked, breaking my train of thought.

"I have a friend who seems to be mixed up in something really bad. I think he's burning thousands of music CDs for an illegal distributor."

Mr. Conner rubbed his beard. "Do you have any evidence?"

"No, but I'm pretty sure my friend is involved. I just don't know if I should tell the police about it."

The computer teacher lowered his head for a minute, then cleared his throat. "That's a tough call, Frank. Maybe you should wait until you're absolutely sure what's going on. You don't want to get your friend in trouble, do you?"

"No. You're right."

I thanked Mr. Conner for his advice and headed off to the science lab. I couldn't concentrate very well, though. For the rest of the school day, one question kept eating away at me.

Who is C. D. Burns?

• • • •

"I don't get it," said my brother. "Why are we here at the Bayview Shopping Mall? You thirsty for an Orange Jupiter?"

"No. We're investigating," I answered.

"Investigating what? A drug deal at Dippy Donuts? A holdup at Hats 'n' Things?"

Joe snickered for a while, then stopped to admire a suede jacket in the window of Checker King.

I grabbed his arm. "Come on. We're here to snoop, not shop."

I started dragging Joe through the mall. A group of teenage girls pointed at us and giggled.

"At least tell me where we're going," he said.

"Do you have Julian's CD with you?"

"Yeah." Joe pulled out his portable player and popped out the CD.

"Where did Julian get the blank CD? What's the brand name?"

Joe studied the label. "Mega Mart."

"And what store are we standing in front of right now?"

Joe looked up. "Mega Mart."

"Congratulations, Joe. You could be a master detective someday."

"And you can be a major dork sometimes."

We gazed up at the giant green Mega Mart sign above the store entrance. The phrase DOUBLE M MEANS DOUBLE SAVINGS glowed in neon lights below the logo.

"The CD section is that way," I said, pushing Joe inside.

We walked past row after row of merchandise, all marked with little signs: REDUCED! and 50% OFF! and SPECIAL CLEARANCE!

"So what do you expect to find here?" Joe asked. "Besides unbelievable bargains."

"I want to talk to a manager," I explained. "I want to know if anyone has been buying blank CDs in bulk."

"What about the CDs stolen from the school?"

"I don't know what to think. Maybe it really *was* a shipping error. Julian used a Mega Mart CD, after all, to burn that music for you."

We reached the music CD section—and were instantly accosted by a creepy-looking manager with thinning hair and an oily mustache.

"Are you boys here for the Mega Madness sale?"

"Mega Madness?"

"Twice the music for half the price!"

"No. We're here to ask you—"

"It's for a limited time only."

"Cool, but I just—"

"You just can't beat our prices. They're the lowest around!"

I wanted to scream. The guy sounded like an angry bulldog.

I glanced at his tag. Next to his gruesome ID photo were the words ARTIE J. KLUMP, MANAGER, CD & DVD SALES.

"Excuse me, Mr. Klump? Mr. Klump!"

Finally I got his attention.

"Yes, sir."

"I'm doing an article for my school paper about illegal CD burning. I just wondered if a lot of high school kids come here to buy blank CDs."

Mr. Klump looked at me as if I were insane. "Of course they come here! We have the lowest prices around! Guaranteed!"

Then he tried to sell us the new Britney CD.

"Excuse me, Mr. Klump!" I said, interrupting him again. "Have you noticed any high school kids buying an unusually large amount of blank CDs?"

He seemed annoyed by my question.

"No!" he barked at us. "Nothing unusual. Nothing unusual at all! HEY, YOU!"

He turned his attention to a young stock boy unloading crates of blank CDs from a pushcart.

"What are you doing with those?" the manager

yelled. "Take those CDs back to the stockroom! They're reserved! TAKE THEM BACK! NOW! MOVE IT!"

The stock boy trembled and fumbled with the boxes, reloading the pushcart as fast as he could.

Joe and I stared at Mr. Klump.

Sweat was pouring down his face and practically dripping from his mustache. The guy was absolutely fuming.

SUSPECT PROFILE

Name: Artie J. Klump

Hometown: Bayport

Physical description: Thirty-six years old, 5'7", 200 lbs. or so, dark thinning hair, mustache.

Occupation: Mega Mart manager, CD and DVD sales

Background: Riverside Business School dropout.

Suspicious behavior: Avoided questions about blank CD purchases, flew into a rage when stock boy brought out cases of "reserved" CDs.

Suspected of: Supplying blank CDs for illegal trade.

Possible motives: Extra cash on the side.

Talk about Mega Madness.

After Klump's temper tantrum, it was a relief to leave the music department of Mega Mart. Joe and I worked our way past all the bargain hunters and headed straight for the mall entrance. I couldn't wait to get out.

Joe nudged me when we reached the registers. "Check it out."

He pointed at a tall older man in a black ski cap and raincoat. He stood at the end of the checkout line, holding two large cardboard boxes.

"So?" I said to Joe. "It's too early in the year for a ski cap, but we're not arresting people for fashion crimes."

Joe rolled his eyes. "Look at the box."

I looked. And Joe was right to point him out.

The man had two full cartons of blank CDs.

"Now why would a guy like him buy a thousand blank CDs all at once?" I wondered out loud.

"Maybe he got swept up in the Mega Madness sale," Joe suggested.

"Let's go talk to him."

"What? Wait! What are you going to say?"

"Relax. I'm cool."

"Yeah, right."

I walked over to the registers and got in line behind the man in the ski cap. Joe came and stood next to me. Leaning forward, I gave the man a little push. He shot me a dirty look in return.

"Sorry, sir," I said. "Lost my balance."

He turned back toward the register.

"That's an awful lot of CDs you have there."

He didn't say anything.

"I was wondering what you plan to do with all of those."

The man spun around slowly. He squinted his gray eyes and studied my face for a moment or two.

Then he dropped the boxes on my foot and took off running!

9.
Shop Till You Drop (Dead)

Unbelievable!

For an older dude, Mr. Ski Cap sure could run.

Look at him go!

At first I just stood there staring in shock. But then my brother's howl of pain snapped me out of it.

"My foot!"

The cardboard boxes had split open at Frank's feet, hundreds of CD cases spilling across the floor. I didn't know what to do first—help Frank or chase the running man.

I decided to lend my brother a hand. But—surprise, surprise—he wanted me to carry on with our mission.

"After him, Joe! He's getting away!"

I spun around and charged toward the mall entrance. Unfortunately I slipped on some CDs— and my butt hit the floor.

Real smooth.

I expected Frank to crack a joke or something. But when I looked up he was limping past the cash register and out into the mall.

"Frank! Wait!"

I picked myself up off the floor and bolted after him, nearly knocking over a woman at the Half-Hour Photo booth. Her vacation pictures went fluttering into the air.

"Sorry, lady!"

Sprinting past the Pizza Pit and Shake Shack, I finally managed to catch up with my brother, who was limping as fast as he could.

"He's heading for the other end of the mall," Frank said, wincing. "We've got to catch him before he reaches Renovation Station. We'll never find him in there."

My brother was right. Renovation Station was one of the biggest home improvement stores in the state. I swear it was the size of several football fields.

"Go, Joe! Don't lose sight of him!"

I looked up and spotted Mr. Ski Cap near the fountain. Glancing at me over his shoulder, he swerved around a trash can and ducked behind the Piercing Hut.

I charged after him, full steam ahead. I didn't even see the lady with the baby carriage until it was too late.

Look out!

My feet slammed down inches in front of the moving stroller—and my whole body went soaring, up, up, and over the screaming infant.

Wham.

I landed hard—and stumbled harder—on top of the Plush Planet display. Dozens of tiny stuffed animals showered down on top of me. Pushing a bug-eyed monkey off my face, I scrambled to my feet and raced toward the Piercing Hut.

Here I come, Mr. Ski Cap.

Crouching down, I circled around the safari-style booth, ready to wrestle the guy to the ground.

Where'd he go?

"Need your ears pierced, sir?"

A young woman with a tube top and navel ring held up her piercing gun.

"Two-for-one sale," she said with a smile.

"Did you see a guy in a black ski cap?" I asked.

She stopped smiling. "Yeah. He went into Sportz Nutz."

She pointed at a small sporting goods store about

forty feet away. Its sign featured cartoon peanuts with arms and legs playing basketball, golf, and other sports. I dashed to the entrance and stopped.

I need backup. Where's Frank?

I glanced back to see my brother limping after me. He opened his mouth to say something, but I held a finger to my lips. Nodding toward the store, I tiptoed to the entrance and went inside.

Frank mouthed something silently before I went in. *Be careful.*

Sportz Nutz was overlit, overcrowded, and noisy. But maybe it just seemed that way because of the flat-screen TVs tuned to different sports channels. The roars of cheering fans echoed throughout the store.

Squatting down, I crept slowly along a row of golf clubs and tennis rackets. Then I turned the corner and . . .

Whap!

Mr. Ski Cap jumped out of nowhere, slamming me in the gut with a tennis racket.

"Ooof!"

Doubled over in pain, I watched the man run past me down the aisle. I started off after him.

That's when he started throwing baseball bats at me.

"Think fast, kid!"

I jumped to the side and ducked. One bat clattered to the floor next to me, the other bounced off a golf bag and knocked over a display of tennis balls. With a huge crash, the whole thing collapsed. Hundreds of yellow balls bounced down the aisle.

Mr. Ski Cap laughed.

I gritted my teeth—and went after him.

Two more baseball bats came hurtling through the air.

Man! Why do people keep throwing things at me?

I dodged one bat, then the other. Golf balls and tees went flying everywhere.

Mr. Ski Cap turned around and ran. I darted down the aisle after him, my feet skidding and rolling over the balls on the floor.

"Whoops!"

I was down.

And up again. But I wasn't fast enough.

Mr. Ski Cap bolted out of the store.

He's getting away! Frank's going to kill me.

But no.

Frank was out there waiting for the guy.

"Freeze!"

Riding the back of end of a shopping cart, my brother rolled across the mall like a NASCAR driver racing to the finish line.

BAM!

The front end of Frank's cart plowed right into the man's rear end.

Direct hit!

Even with a bad foot, my brother could kick butt.

"Good job, Frank!" I yelled.

The man rolled on the floor and moaned.

Not wasting any time, Frank hopped off the cart to apprehend the suspect. But then he collapsed from putting all his weight on his injured foot.

"Frank!"

I ran to help—while Mr. Ski Cap made another run for it.

"Frank! Are you okay?"

My brother held his foot with both hands and groaned. I slipped my hands under his arms and propped him up against an Orange Jupiter stand.

"We've got to get that guy, Joe," he said, gasping. "I don't know who is he is, but he's definitely guilty of *something*."

"I'll get him, Frank," I said. "Which way did he go?"

Frank pointed down the mall toward a rainbow-colored storefront. "I think he ducked into the Yarn Barn."

"Okay. Stay here. Rest your foot. I swear I'm going to catch that guy."

I stood up to leave. Just then a blond teenager stuck her head out of the Orange Jupiter stand.

"Frank? Is that you? Are you hurt?"

It was my brother's not-so-secret admirer—Belinda Conrad.

"Drink this, sweetie. It'll help you feel better."

She handed him an extra-large Tangerine Tomato Slush.

Gross.

Turning away in disgust, I hurried off to the Yarn Barn.

"Wait, Joe! I'm right behind you!"

Frank tried to limp after me, but Belinda held him back, trying to force-feed him the orange slush. I suppose she was trying to help.

Whatever. I wasn't about to let Mr. Ski Cap get away.

I turned around and ran to the entrance of the Yarn Barn. I peeked inside.

Where did he go?

Mr. Ski Cap had somehow disappeared amidst all the colored yarn and knitting supplies.

He shouldn't be hard to find. He's wearing all black.

Taking a deep breath, I strolled down the aisle, peering into every bin I passed. There were mountains of rolled yarn, in every color you could imagine.

Hot pink, lemon yellow, lime green . . .

A sweet elderly lady smiled at me as she purchased a shiny new pair of knitting needles.

"Hello, young man. Are you a knitting fan too?" she asked me.

"No, ma'am. Just a knit-wit," I answered.

She giggled like a little girl. I smiled, then went back to inspecting the bins of yarn.

Raspberry red, royal blue, purple plum, filthy dirty black . . .

Wait a minute.

I stopped in my tracks.

Filthy dirty black?

I turned back to the bin of purple yarn.

Yes, there it is.

A single ball of black yarn was half-hidden among the rolled skeins of purple.

Mr. Ski Cap's ski cap.

Slowly I reached inside and . . .

"LEAVE ME ALONE!" the man screamed and jumped out of the bin like a giant jack-in-the-box. Pouncing on top of me, he wrapped loose strands of yarn around and around my neck, cutting into my skin. Then he pulled. Hard.

He's strangling me!

I tried to fight back, but he was just too strong.

I can't breathe!

The yarn dug tighter into my throat.

This is it. I'm going to die.

I probably would have, too—if that sweet elderly woman hadn't jumped on top of us, jabbing the guy with her shiny new knitting needles.

"Ouch! Ouch! Ouch!"

Mr. Ski Cap pushed the woman away and scrambled to his feet, running for the door.

I loosened the yarn around my neck, gasping for air. My head was spinning.

I'll never catch him now.

There was nothing I could do but lie there helplessly on the floor.

He's getting away.

Mr. Ski Cap bounded toward the exit, gaining speed with every step. Faster and faster he charged toward the main entrance—and his only escape. Nothing could stop him now.

Except for the lime green yarn that Frank had stretched across the aisle.

"Whoooah!"

Mr. Ski Cap tripped.

And fell flat on his face.

Frank let go of the yarn and leaped from his hiding place inside one of the bins. Then he threw himself on top of the fallen man. Crawling quickly to my feet, I rushed over to help my brother hold him down.

Mr. Ski Cap growled and thrashed like a wild animal.

But Frank and I weren't about to let him get away.

After a minute or two his arms and legs stopped kicking, and his whole body started to relax. He laid his head back and panted for a while, glaring at us with his cold gray eyes.

"Okay, I give up," he said. "What did I do wrong?"

Besides strangling me?

I bit my lip and answered him.

"Why don't you tell *us*, Mr. Burns."

10.

The Mysterious Mr. Burns

I can't believe this guy.

The man in the ski cap had nearly crushed my foot and strangled my brother—and now he was looking at us like we were crazy.

"Mr. Burns?" he asked. He had a heavy New York accent.

"Yes," said Joe. "C. D. Burns."

The man let out a slow breath of air. Which didn't smell so sweet, by the way.

"You're C. D. Burns, aren't you?" Joe prodded.

"No, I'm not C. D. Burns."

"Yes, you are. You're C. D. Burns and you're paying high school kids to make illegal music CDs for you."

"I told you, kid, I'm not C. D. Burns."

I looked at my brother. "Maybe we should just hand this guy over to mall security, Joe. Or call the cops."

That got him.

"No, wait. I'll talk," he said, glancing around nervously. "What do you want to know?"

"Are you the man they call C. D. Burns?" I asked.

"No."

"What's your name?"

"Lefty Rue. My real name's Liam but everyone calls me Lefty."

"Have you heard of C. D. Burns?"

"Yeah. I work for him. He sends me money to buy blank CDs. Then he tells me where to deliver them."

"Where does he live? How can we find him?"

"I don't know. Really."

"Call the cops, Joe."

Lefty's jaw dropped open. "No! Wait! I'm telling the truth! I have no idea who Burns is or where he lives. I've never even met the guy! Honest!"

"So how does he contact you?"

"E-mail."

"What's the address?"

Lefty sighed. We waited for his reply, but his mouth was clamped shut.

He wasn't going to tell us.

"Look, Lefty," I said. "We can do this the easy way or the hard way. Which is it going to be?"

He looked at me and scoffed. "Tough guy, huh?" he said. "What are you going to do? Torture me?"

"No," I answered. "But if you give me C. D. Burns's e-mail address, I'll make up a nice, innocent story for the mall security guard who's walking toward us right now."

I had Lefty beat and he knew it.

"Okay, okay," he whispered. "It's music2burn—with a numeral two—at worldbeat dot com."

Just then the security guard came up to us.

"What's the problem here, gentlemen?"

Joe and I crawled off of Lefty and helped him to his feet.

"This is our uncle," I explained to the guard. "We were just playing this little game that we have and, well, I guess it got out of hand."

The security guard glanced at the mess inside the Yarn Barn and nodded his head slowly.

"I see. Well, maybe you boys should play something a little less physical next time. Something like chess or cards."

Joe and I put on our best guilty schoolboy expressions and dropped our heads.

"I think it would be nice if you boys helped the store clerk pick up the merchandise you knocked over," said the guard.

"Yes, sir. We will."

The security guard studied us for moment, then nodded his head again and strolled off down the mall.

Joe and I let out a sigh.

"Come on," I said. "Let's clean up this mess."

We turned back to Lefty.

He was nowhere in sight.

SUSPECT PROFILE

__Name:__ Liam Rue, aka "Lefty"

__Hometown:__ New York City

__Physical description:__ Forty-seven years old, 6'1", 170 lbs., gray hair, seen wearing black ski cap and raincoat.

__Occupation:__ Dockworker, handyman

__Background:__ Served time in prison for attempted robbery with unloaded gun.

__Suspicious behavior:__ Reacted violently when questioned, admitted to delivering blank CDs for man known as C. D. Burns.

__Suspected of:__ Trafficking illegal goods.

__Possible motives:__ Money under the table.

As soon as we got home, Aunt Trudy bombarded us with questions.

"Is that lizard thing still here?"

"Yes, Aunt Trudy," I answered.

"Why haven't you taken him back to the pet store?"

I glanced at Joe.

Talk your way out of this one.

"We were too busy today," he said. "I'll get him out of here first thing tomorrow morning. I promise."

Aunt Trudy shook her head. "You promised to take him back *today*. But he's still here. What does that say about your promises?"

"Not much, I know," Joe admitted. "But don't worry. I'll take care of it."

"You also said you'd take care of that parrot of yours. And who cleans up all the parrot poop in this house?"

"You do, Aunt Trudy."

"And we love you for it," I added, kissing her on the cheek.

"Yes, we do."

Joe planted a kiss on her other cheek.

Aunt Trudy pushed us away. "Oh, knock it off. You boys can't sweet-talk me. Maybe that works on the high school girls, but it won't work on me. Which reminds me, Frank."

"Yes?"

"You got a phone call from Belinda Conrad a few minutes ago."

Oh, no.

"I did?"

"Yes. She wanted to know if you were okay. She said you were limping through the shopping mall tonight. What happened?"

Think fast.

"We were in the sporting goods store and Joe dropped a bowling ball on my foot."

Aunt Trudy gave Joe the eye. "You should be more careful."

Joe rolled his eyes.

We went up to my room, a little tired from the night's adventures. Playback greeted us with a soft squawk and ruffling of feathers. I headed straight for my computer and booted it up.

"Checking to see if you got another e-mail from your girlfriend?" Joe asked, pulling up a chair.

"Belinda Conrad is not my girlfriend."

"She likes you, Frank."

"Yeah, so what am I supposed to do about it?"

Joe shrugged. "I don't know. Like her back?"

I tried to ignore him, turning my attention to the computer screen.

"I'm serious, Frank. Belinda's a great girl. She's smart. She's funny. And in case you haven't noticed, she's totally hot."

Enough already.

I sat back and looked my brother in the eye. "Okay, Joe. You want the truth? I really like Belinda. A lot. But I get too nervous when I'm around her. I never know what to say."

"You should ask her out on a date."

"You should mind your own business."

"But Frank . . ."

"We need to concentrate on the mission, not my love life."

"What love life?"

I pushed him backward until the chair tipped over and dumped Joe onto the floor.

"Hey!"

I went back to my computer. Joe scrambled to his feet and stood up behind me, leaning over my shoulder.

"What are you doing?"

"I'm sending an e-mail to C. D. Burns," I told him.

"Really? What are you going to say?"

"Here. Read it."

Joe leaned closer and started reading.

```
* * * * * * * * * * * * * * * * * * * * * * * * *
* * * OUTGOING TRANSMISSION * * *
* * * * * * * * * * * * * * * * * * * * * * * * *
```

To: music2burn@worldbeat.com
From: iguanaboy@americalink.com
Subject: Business proposal

Message: Hello, Mr. Burns. I'm a student
at Bayport High School. A friend of mine
told me that you're in the business of
duplicating music CDs for the global
market. I would like to offer you my
services. I am very experienced with
computers and fully equipped to burn
large numbers of CDs at your request.
Salary is negotiable. Please let me know
if you're interested. Thank you.

```
* * * * * * * * * * * * * * * * * * * * * * * * *
```

The next morning Joe and I woke up early so we could take the iguana over to Chet Morton's house. Chet was pretty psyched—even though he looked like he'd just crawled out of bed.

"Come on in! I got the old aquarium all fixed up for the little guy."

* * * *

I thought he was going to explode from the excitement. Joe set the cardboard box on the floor, and Chet reached inside to stroke the iguana's head.

"Oh, man! He is *so* cool!"

"Yes. Cold-blooded, in fact," I said. "That's why he needs to have a heat lamp."

"Yeah, I know." Chet pointed to the glass tank in the corner of his room.

Wow. Impressive.

It looked like one of those amazing displays in the Museum of Natural History. Rocks and sand were perfectly arranged around a small pool, with desert plants clustered in the background. Not only did Chet have a heat lamp, he had a whole stack of iguana pet care books next to the tank.

"I think little Iggy, or whatever you want to call him, has found a good home," I said.

Joe and Chet lifted the iguana out of the box and introduced him to his new surroundings. As they tried to get him to eat some lettuce, my eyes wandered to the computer on Chet's desk.

I forgot to check my e-mail.

"Chet? Do you mind if I go online for a second? I need to check my e-mail."

"Knock yourself out."

I sat down at the desk and logged onto the "iguanaboy" account that I'd created last night. A few seconds later I opened the e-mail box.

"Joe. Come here."

We had received an e-mail.

From C. D. Burns.

11.

Playing with Fire

I couldn't believe my eyes.

E-mail from C. D. Burns?

I never thought the mystery man would answer back.

"What does it say?" I asked.

"See for yourself."

I leaned forward and started reading.

```
* * * * * * * * * * * * * * * * * * * * * * * *
* * * INCOMING  TRANSMISSION * * *
* * * * * * * * * * * * * * * * * * * * * * * *


To: iguanaboy@americalink.com
From: music2burn@worldbeat.com
```

Subject: Re: Business Proposal
Message: Thank you for your inquiry.
I am always interested in making new
business contacts. I'd like to start
you off with a small order: 150 copies
of the new album *Ham Sweet Ham* by the
Flaming Pigs. You can find it at your
local music store. I'll pay you fifty
cents per copy plus the cost of the
original CD. Just send me your home
address, and the blank CDs will be
delivered to your doorstep tonight.
C. D. Burns.

* *

"Who's C. D. Burns?" asked Chet, looking over my shoulder.

"That's what we'd like to know," I said.

Chet, as usual, looked confused. He didn't know that we were undercover agents on a secret mission—but he knew we had a habit of digging up trouble.

"C. D. Burns has been paying kids at our school to copy music CDs," Frank explained. "Illegally."

Chet still looked confused. "So who's 'iguana-boy'?"

Frank laughed. "I created a new profile to hide our identities from C. D. Burns."

"Yeah," I said. "And now he's walked right into our trap."

"Or maybe we've walked right into his."

"What do you mean, Frank?"

My brother spun around in the chair. "Burns wants to know our home address. Maybe he suspects we're trying to bust his operation."

I nodded. "You have to admit, we've been asking a lot of people a lot of questions."

"You're right. Burns could be on to us."

"So what should we do?"

"Well, we can't give him our home address."

We sat there silently, trying to plan our next move.

Chet snapped his fingers. "I have an idea," he said. "Give him *my* home address."

Frank shook his head. "It's too dangerous, Chet. What if Burns sends someone to beat you up? Or worse?"

Chet shrugged him off. "I'm not scared," he said. "And anyway, I'm not even going to be here tonight. The family is spending the night at my grandmother's in Philly."

I looked at Frank. "What do you think?"

My brother thought about it. "I don't know, Joe."

"Aw, go ahead," said Chet. "Give him my address. It's okay."

He picked up one of his new pet care books.

"I'm 'iguanaboy' now."

At lunchtime Frank and I hopped on our motorcycles and rode downtown to buy the Flaming Pigs CD. We pulled up in front of a little shop near the bay called Spin City.

A sign in the window said GOING OUT OF BUSINESS.

"That stinks," I said, stepping off my bike. "This place has been here forever."

We went inside and were greeted by Vinnie Spinerelli, a twenty-something hip-hop fan who inherited the place from his rock-and-roller dad.

"Yo, whassup?" he said, tugging on his baseball cap.

"How's it going, Spin?" I replied. Everyone called him Spin.

"I'm good, man." He smirked, then pointed at the sign. "But business is bad."

"I can't believe you're closing, dude," said Frank. "You're the last music store left in town."

Spin grunted and stared down at the counter. "No one comes in here anymore. They get their music on the Internet. Or at a superstore like Mega Mart."

He reached up and ripped a concert poster off the wall, tearing it up in his hands. Frank and I felt bad for the guy. He was about to lose his family business.

"Sorry to hear it, Spin," I said.

"It's no big deal. I've got a few things lined up. I'll be okay. Anyway, what about you guys? Looking for something special?"

"Yeah," said Frank, gazing at the dusty bins of records and CDs. "We're looking for an album called *Ham Sweet Ham* by the Flaming Pigs."

Spin tossed the crumpled poster on the floor. "It hasn't been released yet."

"Really?" I said. "We were told we could get a copy at the local store."

Spin gave another smirk. "I didn't say you couldn't get a copy. I said the album hasn't been released yet."

Reaching underneath the cash register, he pulled out a CD case and slapped it down on the counter. I looked at it. The plastic case featured a cheap photocopied picture of a piggy bank with flames shooting out of the coin slot.

It was *Ham Sweet Ham*.

And it was definitely an illegal bootleg copy.

* * * *

That night Frank got another e-mail from Belinda Conrad.

She wanted to know if he was free tonight. She had an extra ticket to go see "this new band that totally kicks."

The Flaming Pigs.

<u>SUSPECT PROFILE</u>

<u>Name:</u> Vincent Spinerelli, aka "Vinnie" or "Spin"

<u>Hometown:</u> Bayport

<u>Physical description:</u> Twenty-five years old, 5'11", 150 lbs., dark hair and eyes, baggy hip-hop clothes and baseball cap.

<u>Occupation:</u> Bayport High School graduate

<u>Background:</u> Took over father's music store, Spin City.

<u>Suspicious behavior:</u> Displayed anger over losing business to superstores and the Internet, sold us bootleg copy of unreleased Flaming Pigs CD.

<u>Suspected of:</u> Copying and selling illegal music CDs.

<u>Possible motives:</u> Going out of business, needs money.

It figures.

He wrote back: "Sounds cool, Belinda. I wish I could go, but I already have plans for tonight. Sorry. And thanks for asking. Frank."

He was about to send it when I stopped him.

"This is your chance, Frank. Ask her out on a date."

He paused to think about it, then added another line: "P.S. Maybe another time, okay?"

Then he clicked and sent the e-mail.

Not the most romantic message. But for Frank, it was a big step.

"Ready to go?" I asked. "It's starting to get dark outside."

Frank logged off the Internet and grabbed his backpack. "Ready."

He and I headed downstairs and were almost out the door when Dad stopped us.

"Where are you boys heading off to?"

"Top secret, Dad," I said.

Our father knew about our undercover missions for ATAC. Being a former police officer, he was secretly proud—and sometimes worried—about our work. Still, he would occasionally use his connections to help us out.

"Well, I know what it's like to get wrapped up in

a case. But I don't want to see your grades suffer for it. Especially yours, Joe. Don't you have to work on an assignment for computer class?"

I sighed. "Yeah, it's due tomorrow. But don't worry, Dad. Frank's going to help me out."

Our father grunted and nodded and wished us luck. As soon as we left the house, Frank smacked me on the arm.

"So I'm going to help you out, huh?"

"Do you mind, Frank?"

"Nah."

We reached Chet's house in a matter of minutes. The sun was setting behind an apple tree in a neighbor's yard, and the streetlights began to glow with a soft pink light.

"Where's a good spot?" I asked.

Frank scanned the area, looking for a hiding place with a direct view of Chet's front porch. "Right there," he said, pointing across the street. "In those bushes next to the garbage cans."

I cringed. "It's going to stink near the trash."

"It'll stink even more if C. D. Burns catches us."

Reluctantly, I followed Frank into the tall bushes. Ducking down, we hid ourselves in the shadows and began to wait.

We're probably wasting our time, I thought. *He'll*

probably send Lefty to deliver the blank CDs.

Even if that was true, I didn't want to take any chances.

Maybe Burns will take care of this job himself. And take care of us, too.

The sun settled slowly into the horizon. In minutes the whole neighborhood was cloaked in a patchwork of shadows.

"I just thought of something," I said. "What if the CDs aren't dropped off until midnight? Or even later? I can't wait here all night. I have to finish that computer assignment for school."

"That's why I brought this along."

Frank reached into his backpack and pulled out the digital video recorder with night vision. Just as he started setting it up, we heard the sound of something approaching.

It was a dark green pickup truck with a loud muffler.

I froze. "Maybe this is him," I whispered.

The truck crept its way slowly down the street, like some sort of growling animal stalking its prey. Finally it crawled to a stop right in front of us.

"Stay down."

Nothing happened for a while. Frank pushed the record button on the video cam and wedged it between two branches.

Then, very carefully, I raised my head to peek inside the truck.

It was Lefty Rue.

He was wearing the same black ski cap and raincoat he'd worn at the mall. His head was lowered, and I could see he was reading something on a little scrap of paper. Then suddenly he looked up.

I ducked down as fast as I could.

Did he see me?

No. He must have been checking the address on Chet's mailbox, because he shifted the truck into reverse and backed into Chet's driveway.

With the engine still running, he hopped out and reached into the flatbed of the pickup. Grabbing a medium-sized cardboard box, he glanced around to make sure no one was watching. Then he carried the box to the front porch and dropped it on the doorstep.

Frank tugged my arm.

"Joe."

"Shhh."

"I think I heard something. Behind us."

I listened.

Nothing.

Turning my attention back to the house, I watched Lefty jump off the porch and rush back to his truck.

Then I heard it.

The snapping of a twig.

Someone's right behind us.

I tensed up and turned, preparing myself to run, but it was too late.

He found us.

The last thing I saw was a large metal garbage can, shining in the darkness, right over my head.

Bam!

I was knocked out cold.

FRANK

12.

Burned!

It all happened so fast.

My brother collapsed to the ground beside me, crushed beneath the weight of the metal can.

Joe!

Without even thinking, I leaped from the bushes.

And another garbage can hit me in the face.

I went sprawling backward, stumbling over the curb and onto the street.

Man! That hurts!

I must have been stunned by the impact, because all I could do was lay there for a while, breathing in the smell of rotting TV dinners and other trash.

Man! That stinks!

I heard soft footsteps running past me across the street—and then the sound of two men talking.

I couldn't be sure, but I thought one of them said, "I *knew* this was a setup."

A few seconds later I heard two car doors slamming. Then the pickup truck pulled out of Chet's driveway and took off down the street. The sound of the noisy muffler faded away as I pushed the garbage can off me.

A voice whispered from the bushes.

"Frank?"

I ran over and looked down. My brother shifted and groaned beneath a huge heap of trash.

"Joe! Are you okay?"

He gazed up at me, holding his nose. "Dude! I warned you about those garbage cans!"

Reaching down, I helped Joe to his feet. He brushed off some potato chip crumbs and banana peels, then pointed at my forehead.

"You're bleeding, Frank."

I touched the wound and winced. "Just what I need. A scar shaped like a garbage can lid."

"What are you complaining about? I've been knocked out *twice* in this mission."

I was about to throw Joe a pity party when I remembered something.

"The video cam! Maybe it caught a picture of the attacker." I ducked into the bushes and found it lying on the ground. "Or maybe not."

Joe came up next to me. "Hit playback and check it out."

I pressed a button, starting it from the beginning. The small playback screen lit up with a blurry green image of Lefty's truck.

"If nothing else, this proves that Lefty is working for C. D. Burns," I said, watching the man place the cardboard box on Chet's front porch. "Here it comes now. The attack."

Joe leaned in closer for a better view.

Suddenly the image flickered. The camera must have fallen when Joe was hit with the first trash can. The video picture turned on its side, and something filled the screen in a tight close-up.

A pair of white high-top sneakers.

Seconds later the sneakers moved out of the frame. Then the recording ended.

"That's it?" said Joe. "That's all we get to see of C. D. Burns?"

"Yeah, well, it's a clue."

"Not a very good one. Everyone has a pair of sneakers like that."

"We can take a closer look when we get home," I said. "I hooked up the video cam's receiver to my computer. Maybe we can see more detail on a bigger screen."

"You think of everything, Frank. Did I ever tell you you're my hero?"

"Knock it off."

We hurried home and snuck upstairs as quietly as possible. We didn't want to explain our latest injuries to Mom and Dad—or the lingering smell of garbage to Aunt Trudy.

As soon as I sat down at my computer, I saw that I'd received new e-mail.

Joe saw it too.

"Look, Frank! Belinda answered your message! Open it up! Read it! Read it!"

"Later, Joe."

"Aw, come on, Romeo. Why won't you read it?"

"Because we got another message from C. D. Burns."

"We did?"

"Yes. And you know what's scary?"

"What?"

"He didn't send it to iguanaboy. He sent it directly to my home account."

Joe let out a sigh. "He knows who we are."

"Sure looks like it."

"So what does he say?"

I scrolled down and then double-clicked the new e-mail from music2burn@worldbeat.com.

Large capital letters filled the screen:
  STAY OUT OF MY BUSINESS OR YOU'RE GOING TO GET BURNED.

I have to admit, we were beginning to feel a little desperate at this point. Our mission was going badly, and Joe and I both knew it.

The next day at school the question kept eating away at me. *Who is C. D. Burns?*

Class after class, I tried to pay attention, but it was no use. All I could do was study everybody's feet to see what kind of shoes they had on.

I never realized before just how many people wear white high-top sneakers.

Here's just a small sample of the voice memos I recorded that long, horrible day:

"Friday, 8:04 a.m. Saw the following students wearing white high-tops: Craig Spencer, Brenda Sovinski, Rick Pascocello, Liz Perl, Louise Burke, and an unidentified freshman in pigtails."

"Friday, 9:55 a.m. Mr. Conner stops me in the hallway to ask about my head injury. I make up an excuse and look down at his shoes. Black loafers."

"Friday, 10:28 a.m. Principal Foxworth notices the

Band-Aid on my head as I pass his office. Insists that I see the school nurse to make sure I don't need stitches. He is wearing brown suede shoes."

"Friday, 10:36 a.m. Nurse Jones examines me and decides that stitches won't be necessary. As she applies a fresh bandage to my head, I am shocked to notice her white shoes. They are not, however, high-top sneakers."

"Friday, 11:45 a.m. More white-top sightings in cafeteria. Brian Conrad, Chet Morton, Julie Grau . . ."

And so on.

By mid-afternoon, I had listed the names of 248 students and six teachers on my digital recorder. A quarter had worn high tops, and none of those people were teachers.

"You need to chill out, Frank," my brother told me after I played a few of the entries.

"How can I chill out?" I asked. "Burns knows who we are. He knows what we're doing. He even managed to physically attack us, Joe! And we still don't have a clue about his identity!"

"We know who his connections are," Joe reminded me. "And we've gathered evidence linking Julian and Lefty to the case. We could stop right now and let ATAC handle the rest."

I shook my head and readjusted my bandage.

"It's personal now, Joe," I said. "We're going to finish this on our own. We just need another lead."

Joe knew me too well to argue.

The school bell rang. As I headed off to my locker, I kept my head down and my mind focused. I was determined to get Burns. And nothing was going to distract me, not even all the white sneakers I passed in the hall.

"Hi, Frank."

It was a girl in black leather pumps.

"Hi, Belinda."

"What happened to your head?"

"Oh, you know me. Total headbanger. How was the Flaming Pigs show?"

"Absolutely *fantastic*!" she raved. "Have you ever been to the Bitter End? They sell the *coolest* CDs. Stuff you can't find *anywhere*."

I raised an eyebrow. "Really?"

"Yeah, I bought the Pigs' new album there. You ought to hear it."

"Do you have it with you now?"

"Hold on." Belinda reached into her purse. She pulled out a *Ham Sweet Ham* CD.

It was another illegal bootleg copy.

And just the lead I was looking for.

13.

To the Bitter End

I can't believe we're here.

The Bitter End was one of the coolest clubs in the entire state—and the last place I ever expected my uptight brother to take me. Especially on a school night.

"I'm impressed, Frank. This is a pretty serious hangout . . . for a computer geek like you."

My brother pulled off his motorcycle helmet and cleared his throat. "If I were you, Joe, I'd be a little nicer to the so-called geek who's going to help you ace your computer class."

"Good point."

We hopped off our bikes and started crossing the parking lot. The club didn't look like much from the outside—just a big gray concrete-block warehouse.

The sign out front was nothing more than a giant rectangle of glowing white plastic with movable black letters.

THE BITTER END PRESENTS THE FLAMING PIGS WITH PARTY GHOST AND SCALDING HOT WATER. ENDS FRIDAY.

There was a long line at the door. A huge bouncer with a shaved head was checking everyone's IDs.

"We might not be able to get in," said Frank.

"Belinda got in last night," I told him. "And besides, with your leather jacket and messy hair, you look a lot older. Tougher, too. Like someone in a police lineup."

"Thanks, Joe. First I'm a geek, now I'm a gangsta. Which is it?"

"Take your pick," I said. "Either way, it doesn't matter. I know a better way to get in."

I pointed to the side of the club. A small moving van was parked next to a large door, and a couple of big guys were unloading band equipment. On the side of the van someone had painted dozens of little black pig silhouettes against a bright orange background—and the words "Flaming Pigs."

"Follow me," I said. "And try to act cool."

Frank flipped up the collar of his leather jacket.

I rolled my eyes and led the way around the side

of the building, casually strolling up to the van as if we knew where we were going.

"Careful! Don't drop that!" shouted one of the band's crew.

Another crew member, a short, skinny guy, struggled with a huge amplifier. I nodded at Frank.

"We got it, buddy," I said, jumping to his aid.

Frank and I lifted the amplifier up off the ground and carried it inside the club.

"See?" I whispered. "We're in."

Of course, to make it seem like we were supposed to be there, Frank and I had to help the crew unload the entire van. It was a small price to pay— especially when we got to meet the Flaming Pigs.

"Thanks, guys," said Luke Ripper, the legendary lead singer.

I immediately recognized him from the band's album covers. The long black hair, ripped sleeveless shirt, and blue-tinted shades were his trademarks.

"No problem, man," I said. "I'm a huge fan. *Everybody Pig Out* is a classic. Everyone at our school's crazy for it."

"Really?" said Luke, a little surprised. "That's news to us. Our record company said nobody's buying our albums."

Frank looked at me, then turned to Luke.

"That's weird," he said. "A friend of mine

bought your new CD last night, right after your show, here at the club."

Luke Ripper pounded his fist against the wall and looked at his bandmates. "Did you hear that, guys? That little club rat is selling our new album here."

"It's not even in stores yet," said Bam-Bam, the drummer. Bam-Bam always had a baffled look on his face, even when he was pounding out a song.

"We should kick that bootlegger's butt," added Grunt, the guitarist. Grunt was the wild one of the group.

Soon the whole band was shouting and arguing. I was afraid they were going to start throwing things.

The Pigs are flaming mad.

Frank tried to calm everybody down.

"Before you start any trouble, I should let you in on a secret," he said. "My brother and I are undercover agents. We're cracking down on a worldwide crime ring that's copying your music."

"No way," said Luke. "That kind of stuff drives us crazy. We're barely making enough to put gas in our van."

"Yeah," said Bam-Bam. "Did you see our van? The thing's falling apart."

Frank nodded. "We're trying to catch the people

who're skimming your profits. But we need your help."

Luke Ripper took a deep breath, then looked around at his band. "What do you say? Should we help these guys burn the burners?"

"I'm in," said Bam-Bam.

"Me too," Grunt agreed.

"Okay, then," said Frank. "First we need to find the man behind it all. Tell me about this 'little club rat' you mentioned. Who is he?"

Just then the stage door burst open with a loud bang.

In walked a short, paunchy man with a white ponytail and stubby cigar. He wore a black Bitter End T-shirt and a baseball cap with the word MANAGER on it.

"Flaming Pigs! You're up next! Move it!"

Luke Ripper shot us a look and nodded toward the man. Instantly, I knew it was him.

The club rat.

"Why are all these people backstage?" the rat complained. He fixed his eyes on Frank and me. "Do you boys have backstage passes?"

"They're cool, Tom," said Luke. "They're with us."

The manager studied us and sneered. "Well, they need to get passes. Just like that crew member of yours poking around the stage a few minutes ago. He said he had to set up a 'special light show.' I told him to get a pass or there ain't gonna be a show at all."

"A special light show?" said Luke. He looked confused.

The manager held up his hand.

"You got five minutes, Pigs."

Then he turned and left, slamming the door behind him.

Luke Ripper looked at us and smirked. "Guess who that was."

"The club rat," I said.

"Yeah. His name's Tom Start and he's a total sleazebag."

"I hear he records our concerts to make bootleg CDs," said Bam-Bam.

"I want to get that guy," Grunt growled.

Luke shook his head. "I think Tom might be totally losing it. I mean, what was he ranting and raving about? We don't have a special light show."

I looked at Frank.

"Maybe someone is trying to sabotage the show," I said.

Everybody looked at me.

I continued. "Tom Start could be C. D. Burns, the man behind the illegal CD burning. Maybe

121

he's afraid you'll find out about all the copies he's made of your music. Maybe he's trying to get rid of you."

The Flaming Pigs mulled it over.

"I think you boys are watching too much TV," said Luke finally. "I also think the band should get out there and play."

Nodding in agreement, they picked up their instruments and headed for the stage.

"Wait, Luke," said Frank. "I really think you should cancel the show."

The lead singer stopped in his tracks. He smiled at us over his shoulder. "Haven't you ever heard the expression, boys? The show must go on."

Then he walked out on the stage.

The crowd went crazy.

As the Flaming Pigs launched into their first song, Frank and I worked our way toward the audience. We had to squeeze through a mass of screaming fans, jumping up and down in Flaming Pigs concert shirts.

Frank tugged my arm and pointed.

Everyone was holding *Ham Sweet Ham* CDs with homemade covers.

Bootleg copies.

Frank stopped and asked a girl with green hair where she got her CD.

"Back there!" she yelled over the music. "Under the counter! You have to ask for it!"

Frank looked at me, then pushed forward through the crowd. Soon we reached the back of the club.

"Joe! Look!"

I looked.

A few feet away, Tom Start stood inside a large black booth filled with concert shirts and CDs. He was selling stuff like nobody's business, reaching beneath the countertop, swapping twenty-dollar bills for the Pigs' new CD.

Frank and I pushed closer to the booth.

When we got to the front of the line, Tom Start looked up at us—and froze.

"What do you want?" he snarled.

"We want the Flaming Pigs to get the money they deserve," I answered back.

"What are you talking about?"

"The bootleg CDs, Mr. Start," said Frank. "They're illegal."

The guy's mouth dropped open. Then his whole face turned red.

"Get out of here! NOW!" he shouted.

Frank and I held our ground.

"You're in a lot of trouble, Start," I said.

He didn't answer me.

Instead he began jumping up and down, waving his arms over our heads. "Bubba! Jack! Over here! Get 'em!"

Frank and I turned around.

Two huge bouncers tackled us to the floor.

POW.

Frank and I went down so fast we barely knew what hit us.

The bouncer named Bubba—or maybe it was Jack—knocked me to the floor and pinned me down with all his body weight.

And I'm talking *serious* body weight—two hundred and fifty pounds at least.

No doubt about it. These guys were total giants and Frank and I were dead meat.

We barely had a chance to catch our breath when the bouncers hoisted us off the floor and dragged us to the exit. We kicked and fought them every step of the way—even yelled for help—but it was no use. The audience was rocking out to the music of the Flaming Pigs.

The bouncers flung open the exit door. Struggling, I looked up and spotted Luke Ripper on the stage. "Luke!"

The lead singer gazed out over the crowd, squinting his eyes.

Yes! He sees us!

SUSPECT PROFILE

Name: Tom Start

Hometown: Atlantic City, NJ

Physical description: Forty-one years old, 5'7", 165 lbs., long white hair, tattoos on both arms, smokes cigars.

Occupation: Bitter End nightclub manager, band promoter

Background: Father used to gamble. Grew up with ten dogs.

Suspicious behavior: Sold bootleg copies of Flaming Pigs CD, told bouncers to boot us from club.

Suspected of: Being the real "C. D. Burns."

Possible motives: Money, lots of it.

But there was nothing he could do, because as soon as he hit his final note, the "special light show" began.

White-hot sparks shot out of a pair of flashpots at Luke's feet.

And the stage burst into flames.

14.

Band on the Run

At first everyone thought the fire was part of the show.

But Joe and I knew better.

C. D. Burns did this.

Foot-high flames danced across the stage, forcing Luke Ripper to jump back a few feet. The crowd went crazy. And who could blame them? They thought it was just a special effect.

Until the curtains caught on fire.

This doesn't look good.

Bam-Bam stopped drumming. Grunt ran to the edge of the stage and started beating back the flames with his guitar. Luke Ripper tried to help him but only managed to make the mess worse.

There must be gasoline or something on the stage.

126

The flames leaped higher, and smoke started to fill the club.

Someone screamed.

"We're going to die!"

Bubba and Jack jumped into action. Shoving Joe and me aside, the bouncers rushed into the club, waving their arms like traffic cops.

"Stay calm, everybody! Make your way to the exits! Just stay calm!"

Right.

The crowd went nuts. The whole place erupted in a loud chorus of hacking, coughing, and screams.

"Frank! Look!"

Joe pointed toward the stage. The band scrambled to the center of the stage, surrounded by flames. Luke Ripper hopped up and down, slapping his legs with his hands.

What's he doing?

Then it hit me: His jeans were on fire.

"We've got to help them!" Joe shouted.

I definitely agreed.

But when we tried to run toward the stage, we were nearly trampled by a howling mob. Pushing and shoving, they sent us reeling back until we slammed against a pair of columns, struggling to keep from falling to the floor.

Hold on.

I couldn't see Joe. But I knew where he was heading. Pushing against the flow of screaming people, I moved closer and closer to the stage.

I coughed and wiped my eyes.

All I could see were smoke and flames.

Then, taking a deep breath, I hurled myself out of the crowd.

And into the fire.

Pulling my shirt up over my mouth, I took a few steps forward and looked around frantically. The flames were spreading through the whole club now, blazing up the walls and licking the ceiling.

"Joe! Where are you? Joe!!!"

Answer me. Please.

"Frank! Over here!"

Thank you.

My brother's voice rang out from the stage. I ducked down below the thick haze of smoke and rushed forward, trying not to breathe.

There he is.

Joe crouched down on the stage next to Grunt and Bam-Bam. They were all leaning over Luke Ripper, who was curled up in a ball, coughing and coughing.

Smoke inhalation.

We had to get him out of there. And fast.

Jumping onto the stage, I hopped over some flames and joined the others.

"Let's carry him," I said. "Help me pick him up."

The four of us reached beneath Luke's shaking body and hoisted him up.

"Which way?" asked Bam-Bam.

Joe pointed toward the nearest exit at the front of the club. We were able to move pretty quickly off the stage. With four people carrying him, Luke wasn't very heavy.

Then one of the ceiling beams collapsed.

Whoomp!

Right in front of us, it sent a fluttering of sparks and ashes flying. We tried moving around the fallen beam but found ourselves face-to-face with a roaring wall of fire.

"We're trapped," Grunt muttered.

He was right. The entire front of the nightclub was engulfed in flames. Raising my head, I searched desperately for an escape.

"Let's go backstage!" I shouted.

Circling around the blaze, we carried Luke down a narrow corridor toward a steel door. The burning curtains crashed to the floor behind us.

"This way!" yelled Bam-Bam.

The drummer pushed open the door, took a step forward, and stopped. I took a quick look around.

We were in the room where we'd unloaded the band equipment—through the side door of the club.

It's our only chance.

There was just one problem.

The whole room was in flames.

Just our luck.

"Looks like a dead end, guys," Grunt grunted.

"We can't give up," I said.

"We can't walk through fire, either," he said.

Joe spun around, glancing behind us. "Wait right here," he said. "Hold on to Luke."

My brother broke away from us and headed back into the club.

What are you doing, Joe?

With a running leap, he jumped and dove over the burning beam. For a second he disappeared into the fire. Then he crashed to the floor on the other side of the beam, rolling and coughing.

Dude!

The ceiling crackled overhead. Flaming chunks of the building showered down to the floor.

Look out!

Joe scrambled out of the way in the nick of time.

Man, that was close.

Throwing himself against the side wall, he inched his way forward, then stopped and reached out for something.

I squinted my eyes to see through the smoke.

It was an emergency fire hose.

All right, Joe! Do it!

My brother grabbed the heavy-duty hose and pulled hard until it unraveled at his feet. Then he reached for the round steel handle to turn on the water.

"Aauuugh!"

Joe snatched his hand away. The fire must have heated up the steel.

But that didn't stop him.

Tearing off his T-shirt and wrapping it around his hand, he grabbed the handle and gave it hard twist.

Nothing happened at first.

Then, with a loud sputter, the hose wriggled like a snake—and sprayed a huge gush of water into the air.

He did it!

Joe bent down and grabbed it, aiming the nozzle toward the ceiling beam on the floor. Slowly the water drenched the burning wood, dousing enough of the flames for him to step safely over and make his way back toward us.

"Move back!" he yelled.

Grunt, Bam-Bam, and I lifted Luke up and moved out of the doorway to let Joe through. Holding the hose like a machine gun, he fought off the flames a few feet at a time.

"Follow him!" I shouted to the others. "And stay close!"

Step by step we made our way across the blazing room, closer and closer to the side door. Luke coughed and groaned in our arms.

We're running out of time.

Shuffling through the ashes—and trying not to breathe in the smoke—we finally reached the exit door. Joe kicked it open with a loud bang.

And we were free.

Way to go, Joe!

The cool night air never felt better. We all gasped and sucked it into our lungs as deeply as we could.

Joe dropped the hose and helped us carry Luke Ripper away from the burning building.

"There's an ambulance!" I pointed out.

We moved quickly toward the flashing lights across the parking lot. There were fire trucks and emergency vehicles pulling up to every corner.

A couple of paramedics rushed to our aid. "We'll take care of him," one of them said, leaning over Luke. "He's going to be okay. The rest of you join the others over there."

He nodded toward the front of the building, where a large group of survivors were huddled together under blankets, coughing and staring with stunned eyes at the burning nightclub.

Bam-Bam shook his head and nudged Grunt.

"Now that's what I call a light show."

* * * *

Twenty minutes later the firefighters had everything under control. Every last flame was put out, and the club was a blackened shell.

"It looks like everybody got out," one of the firemen said to another. "Other than a few mild cases of smoke inhalation, no one got hurt."

I looked around and scanned the crowd.

Where's Tom Start?

"I don't see that sleazeball manager," said Joe.

"I was thinking the same thing."

"Maybe he got trapped inside the booth."

Before I could stop him, my brother bolted past the firefighters and ran into the building.

"Joe!" I yelled after him.

I dashed after him, ignoring the protests of one of the firemen. Stumbling through the charred wreckage, I headed for the back of the club where Tom Start had been selling his illegal CDs.

"Out of the way!" someone yelled.

I ran up behind Joe and froze.

Two firefighters pushed past us, carrying a white stretcher with a body on it. We looked down to see a man lying on his back, clenching a fistful of money.

It was Tom Start.

And he was dead.

15.

Dead or Alive

I couldn't believe it.

Burns got burned.

I watched a paramedic cover Tom Start's face with a sheet before taking him outside.

It's all over.

"Man, what a way to end the mission," I said to Frank. "Our prime suspect gets killed before we even had a chance to prove anything. C. D. Burns is dead."

Frank looked me in the eye. "C. D. Burns isn't dead, Joe."

"What are you talking about?"

"Think about it," he said. "Why would Tom Start burn down his own club?"

"To cover his tracks," I answered. "He wanted to

destroy the evidence. He had thousands of bootleg CDs here, and he knew we were on to him."

"But remember—right before the Flaming Pigs went onstage, Tom Start mentioned a guy setting up a 'special light show.'"

"Yeah, so?"

"He thought it was one of the band's crew," Frank continued. "But it wasn't. It was C. D. Burns."

"Why would Burns do this?"

Frank looked down, thinking. "He knows what we're up to, Joe. By burning down the club, he could hide his connections to Tom Start, the bootleg CDs, even the band he was ripping off—all at the same time."

I glanced at the devastation around us and shook my head.

"The guy must be crazy," I said.

"We've got to catch him, Joe. And fast. He might go after Julian and Lefty next, just to shut them up."

I looked across the club—and spotted something.

"Look, Frank. There's something under the booth."

Running over to the burnt structure, I knelt down and pulled out a flat metal box. I opened it up.

Man!

The box was filled with cash—probably thousands of dollars, bundled together with rubber bands. One of the stacks had a little piece of paper attached.

Written on it were the words: FOR C. D. BURNS.

"See? This proves it," said Frank, ducking down. "Tom Start was selling CDs for Burns."

Behind us a firefighter yelled, "Hey! What are you kids doing in here? Get out! It's dangerous!"

Frank grabbed the metal box, tucked it into his leather jacket, and zipped it up.

"Sorry. We thought we could help," he said, standing up and facing the fireman.

"You could help by going outside."

"Yes, sir."

We slipped past him and went out to the parking lot.

"Frank! Joe!"

It was Luke Ripper. The long-haired lead singer was up on his feet, leaning against Bam-Bam and Grunt next to an ambulance.

"Luke!" I shouted, happy to see he was okay. "How's it going, man?"

"I'm cool, dude," he said with a shrug. "But my jeans are burnt to a crisp."

He raised a leg to show off the charred remains of his ripped pants.

"Hey, they look good like that!" said Bam-Bam.

"Yeah, man. Maybe we should all burn our clothes," said Grunt. "We *are* the Flaming Pigs, after all."

Frank and I snickered.

Then we told them about Tom Start.

The band stopped laughing. Luke Ripper looked down at the ground and frowned. "The guy was a major jerk," he said. "But he didn't deserve to die like that."

Frank told them his theory about Start's fatal connection to C. D. Burns and showed them the metal box filled with cash.

"We still need to catch him," my brother said. "And I think we can use this money to lure him out of hiding."

Luke threw his arm over Frank's shoulder. "Well, if you guys need our help, let us know. You saved my life, dudes. I owe you. Big-time."

I could see the wheels turning in Frank's head.

"Do the Flaming Pigs have a Web site?" he asked.

Well, it turned out that the Pigs *did* have a Web site—and they were willing to share their private access codes with us.

"What are you planning to do, Frank?"

I pulled up a chair next to my brother and his computer. Playback flew around the bedroom, trying to get our attention, but we ignored him.

Sorry, bird. We have a killer to catch.

Frank started typing on the keyboard. "I'm going to pretend to be Luke Ripper," he explained. "And I'm going to send C. D. Burns a message."

He finished typing, then leaned back so I could read the message:

```
* * * * * * * * * * * * * * * * * * * * * * * *
* * * O U T G O I N G   T R A N S M I S S I O N * * *
* * * * * * * * * * * * * * * * * * * * * * * *
```

To: music2burn@worldbeat.com
From: ripper@theflamingpigs.com
Subject: Tom Start

Message: Hello, Mr. Burns. You don't know me. I'm Luke Ripper, the lead singer of the Flaming Pigs. Last night there was a fire at the Bitter End. The manager, Tom Start, was killed. I found your name and e-mail in a metal box he kept in his booth. I thought you might want to know about his unfortunate death.
Signed, Luke Ripper.

* *

Frank clicked and sent the message.

"Do you think he'll answer?" I asked.

Frank shrugged. "He will if he wants to get his hands on the money."

Two minutes later a message was sent back to the Web site in response to the e-mail.

Frank clicked it open. We huddled closer to the screen and read C. D. Burns's reply.

* *
* * * INCOMING TRANSMISSION * * *
* *

To: ripper@theflamingpigs.com
From: music2burn@worldbeat.com
Subject: Re: Tom Start

Message: Yes, I heard about the fire.
What a tragedy. Tom Start was a very
shrewd businessman, and he will be
missed. I know this may sound a bit
cold and uncaring, but I can't help
wondering if he'd left anything for
 me inside that metal box. He owes
 me quite a bit of money, you see.

Please let me know. It's very important.
Signed, C. D. Burns.

* *

Yes! It worked!
"What do we do now?" I asked Frank.
"Simple," he said. "We arrange a meeting to give him his money. I want to see if C. D. Burns is who I think he is."
"You have a theory?"
Frank nodded and started typing another message.
"Well? Who is it?" I asked.
Ignoring me, Frank finished his reply. I leaned over to read it.

* *
* * * O U T G O I N G   T R A N S M I S S I O N * * *
* *

To: music2burn@worldbeat.com
From: ripper@theflamingpigs.com
Subject: Re: Re: Tom Start

Message: As a matter of fact, Mr. Burns, there is money in the box, and it has your name on it. I just wanted to make

sure you were the right guy before I
handed over $10,000. How can I get it
to you?
Signed, Luke Ripper.

* *

Clicking the mouse, Frank sent the message.

I took a deep breath and waited.

Playback flew over my head and landed on top
of the computer screen. I guess he wanted to see
what we were so interested in.

When the e-mail response flashed on the Web
page with a loud *bling,* the parrot squawked and
flapped his wings. He even tried to imitate the
sound.

"Bling! Bling! Bling!"

Frank clicked open the message and read it out
loud.

* *
* * * INCOMING TRANSMISSION * * *
* *

To: ripper@theflamingpigs.com
From: music2burn@worldbeat.com
Subject: Re: Re: Re: Tom Start

```
Message: You can bring the money to my
warehouse tomorrow night at eight
o'clock. It's located at the Bayport
docks, the last pier on the south end.
I'll be waiting for you.
Signed, C. D. Burns.
```

* *

That was it.

Mission accomplished.

The Hardy brothers were finally going to meet Mr. Burns face-to-face.

"Good job," I said, slapping Frank on the back. "Your plan worked like a charm."

He turned off his computer and spun around in his chair.

I didn't like the look on his face.

"It's not over yet, Joe."

"What are you talking about? You just set up the perfect sting."

"I don't know," he said grimly. "What we're doing is pretty dangerous."

"Hey. We live for danger, remember?"

Frank stood up and started pacing. "Yeah, but we also have to remember to be careful."

There were those words again.

Be careful.

"Don't worry, Frank," I assured him. "We're up for the job."

Frank stopped pacing. "If we blow this, Joe, *we'll* be the ones who get burned."

Playback picked up on his final word, flapping and squawking so loudly it scared me a little.

"Burned! Burned! Burned!"

16.

Facing the Music

The whole family suspected something was up.

When we tried to leave the house the following night, Aunt Trudy stopped us to ask where we were going. Dad wanted to know how Joe's computer class was going. And Mom wondered if I had a date with Belinda.

Sheesh.

"Enough with the questions!" I said. "It's Saturday night. Can't a couple of guys have a little fun without being interrogated?"

"Yeah," Joe added. "Don't you trust us?"

Aunt Trudy narrowed her eyes and raised a finger. "We trust that you boys are smart enough to stay out of trouble. If I have to mend another pair

144

of ripped pants, I swear, you're going to have to face the music."

Joe smirked. "As long as it's not Frank Sinatra."

Laughing, we charged out the door and hopped on our motorcycles. Just before we headed off to meet the mysterious C. D. Burns, Joe turned to me and winked.

"*Someone's* going to face the music tonight."

It was totally dark by the time we reached the docks. No moon. No stars. Just a cold inky haze hung over the wooden piers, dimming the streetlights over our heads.

We rode our bikes to the last warehouse and stopped.

"This is it," I said.

As soon as we killed our engines, I started to get nervous. Maybe it was the creepy sound of the waves softly slapping the piers.

Or maybe it's because Burns is going to try to kill us tonight.

I pushed the thought from my mind. Grabbing the metal cash box, I turned around and studied the warehouse along the pier.

Where are you, Mr. Burns?

The warehouse wasn't about to reveal its secrets.

In fact, the blank square building hid its face behind a mask of shadows.

Come out, come out, wherever you are.

Joe threw his arm around me. "What do you say, bro? Ready to do this?"

"Ready as ever. Let's go."

Our footsteps echoed across the wooden planks as we made our way down the pier. And my heart pounded louder with every step.

"I think I see him," Joe whispered.

I peered through the darkness.

Yes, there he is.

At the corner of the warehouse, standing beneath a low overhang, was a tall figure.

C. D. Burns.

I clutched the cash box tighter in my hands. Then, taking a deep breath, Joe and I walked over to greet the man.

"You boys should be more careful," said a deep voice.

Joe and I stopped.

The man took two steps out of the shadows. The first thing I could see in the dull light were his shoes.

White high-top sneakers.

Then his face came into view.

Joe gasped.

"Mr. Conner! You? You're C. D. Burns?"

The high school computer teacher took another step closer, chuckling softly.

"Of course I'm not C. D. Burns," he said. "I just came here to make sure Burns didn't hurt you boys."

Yeah, right.

"Let me explain. I knew you were coming to meet him here because I tapped into your computer, Frank," Mr. Conner continued. "I was worried you were messing around with a dangerous criminal."

"You're lying," I said. "You're C. D. Burns, and I can prove it."

The teacher stopped and frowned. "What do you mean, Frank?"

I pulled the digital sound recorder from my pocket and pushed the play button.

Lefty's voice crackled from the tiny speaker: "What happened, Mr. C?"

Another voice answered him: "I knocked the boys out, just to scare them. I *knew* this was a setup! Now let's get out of here."

I pushed the stop button.

Mr. Conner glared at me.

"I slipped the wireless microphone into Lefty's pocket at the mall," I explained. "I recorded everything on the night you attacked us, but it was hard to recognize your voice because you were whispering. But I got it."

Mr. Conner didn't try to argue.

Instead he pulled out a knife.

"Hand over the recorder," he snarled.

I reached out and gave it to him. With a quick toss, he threw the device over the side of the pier. I heard it land in the water with a tiny splash.

"Okay," he said. "Now give me the money."

I sighed and handed him the metal cash box.

"Stand back," he warned, waving the knife in the air.

Joe and I stepped back while Mr. Conner opened the box. He glanced down at a stack of papers and growled.

"What's this?"

"My computer class assignment," said Joe. "I know it's a little overdue, but I haven't been able to finish it. Sorry about that."

Mr. Conner howled. "WHERE'S MY MONEY?"

Throwing the box of papers to his feet, he lunged at us with the knife.

Joe and I ducked out of the way, jumping back in opposite directions. Mr. Conner raised the knife again.

But this time, he was forced to choose just one of us.

Which happened to be me.

"You're dead, kid!"

He swiped at my chest with the knife, slicing through the air and grazing my leather jacket.

I staggered and fell.

Mr. Conner sneered. "I'll give you an A for effort, Frank. But this is one lesson you're going to fail."

The teacher leaped at me with the knife.

I scrambled backward like a crab until I reached the end of the pier. Teetering on the edge, I heard the soft waves gurgling beneath me.

Mr. Conner pointed his knife like a sword.

"I've heard you like to solve mysteries, Hardy. Well, this time you've really gone overboard."

He jabbed at my throat. I tilted my head back—and prepared to plunge over the side—when somebody yelled, "Hey! Conner! Burn *this*!"

Joe jumped up behind his teacher. He swung the metal cash box through the air and clobbered Mr. Conner in the head.

Nice swing, Joe!

The man was stunned. Knocked down by the blow, he moaned and dropped his knife.

"Joe! His knife!" I shouted.

Joe looked down and gave the weapon a quick kick, sending it clattering across the planks. Then he started walking toward me. "Are you okay, Frank?"

"Joe! Behind you!"

My brother spun around, but it was too late.

The crazed teacher charged across the pier.

And shoved Joe over the edge.

No!

The sound of the splash chilled me to the bone. I could only imagine how chilled my brother was by the shock of the cold water.

Good thing he's a good swimmer.

But I had to stop worrying about Joe.

Because Mr. Conner was coming after *me* now.

And worse yet, he had the knife.

I decide to make a run for it. Turning toward the shore, I bolted across the pier, but I didn't get very far. Something was holding me back.

It was Conner, of course.

He had me by the leather jacket.

"Where are you going, Frank?" he snapped. "School is still in session."

With a sharp tug, he pulled me back against him. With one arm he grabbed my waist. And with the other, he pressed the cold blade of the knife against my throat.

"I told you that you were going to get burned," he whispered in my ear.

I froze and gasped for air, the blade pressing against my skin.

"You'll never get away with this," I said.

"Sure I will. I threw your evidence into the bay."

"I made copies of it. You know all about copies, don't you, Mr. Conner?"

He scoffed. "But you said you couldn't recognize my voice."

"Not at first. But we have video evidence that proves it was you."

"Video evidence?"

"I filmed it during the attack," I said. "I have pictures of your shoes."

"My shoes?"

Mr. Conner pulled away from me to glance down at his sneakers. White high tops. Sure, there were lots of other white high tops in town—but these bought me some time

This is my chance.

I knocked his arm away from my throat. Ducking fast, I pulled myself free and darted to the side.

Mr. Conner was furious.

"That's it, Hardy. Prepare to die!"

Raising the knife over his head, he ran and leaped and . . .

POW!

Three men jumped out of the shadows and tackled him.

I couldn't believe my eyes.

It was the Flaming Pigs!

Luke Ripper, Bam-Bam, and Grunt wrestled the knife away from Mr. Conner and pinned him down to the pier.

"We got him, Frank!" Luke yelled over his shoulder.

"Wha—what are you guys doing here?" I asked.

"Never mind us," said Grunt. "Go check on your brother."

Joe!

I ran to the edge of the pier and looked over the side.

Nothing. Just blackness and gentle waves.

"Joe! Can you hear me? Joe!"

I stopped screaming and listened.

"Don't just stand there, Frank. Help me up."

It was Joe.

He was six feet below me, bobbing up and down in the water, clinging to one of the beams beneath the pier.

"Hello? I'm waiting."

By the time we managed to get my brother out of the water, the police had arrived.

"I called 9-1-1 as soon as we saw that guy pull the knife on you," said Bam-Bam, waving his cell phone.

Joe shivered under a police blanket. "But why